Exotic Savory Cuisine

from

Around the World

By

Lola Abiodun-Adegoke

 www.trafford.com

North America & international
toll-free: 1 888 232 4444 (USA & Canada)
phone: 250 383 6864 ♦ fax: 250 383 6804 ♦ email: info@trafford.com

The United Kingdom & Europe
phone: +44 (0)1865 487 395 ♦ local rate: 0845 230 9601
facsimile: +44 (0)1865 481 507 ♦ email: info.uk@trafford.com

10 9 8 7 6 5 4 3 2 1

Dedication

This cookbook is dedicated to the loving memory of my dear Father – Mr. Johnson Olawole, who taught me the way that I should go in life; my dear Mother – Mrs. Susannah Olawole, who allowed me to use her kitchen to learn.

About the Author

Lola Abiodun-Adegoke is an accomplished Management Consultant and a freelance proofreader with an international background having lived and worked in three continents: Europe, Africa and America.

During her successful career that spans multiple industries in private and public sectors, she developed relationships with individuals from more than 30 countries that taught her about diversity in cultures and how food is a critical distinguishing element in all cultures.

Lola sits on the board of Directors for a family Hotel business in Nigeria, a Hotel Management and Catering School in Nigeria. The hotel won the 1987 MAGGI National Cooking competition in Nigeria. As an undergraduate, Lola also worked in the hotel during Easter and Christmas peak periods, assisting the head chef.

Prior to being a Management Consultant, Lola was a successful entrepreneur and prior to her entrepreneurial venture, she worked as a Civil Servant at the Lord Chancellor's Office in England. Lola has an MBA from Cardiff Business School, University of Wales, UK and a Bachelor's degree with honors from University of Ilorin, Nigeria. She is married with two beautiful children and lives in Atlanta.

Acknowledgement

One person without the input of others cannot write an international cookbook in its entirety. There are diverse recipes, delicacies and cooking techniques in all continents, that one person can't possibly learn everything there is to know about cooking. For this reason, the suggestions and guidance of many people that enjoy eating good food have gone into the making of this cookbook.

I give God all the glory for blessing me with cooking skills in other to be a blessing to all that use this cookbook.

I especially would like to thank my mother –Mrs. Susannah Olawole for her encouragement, willingness and diligence in teaching me how to cook from a very young age. She taught me how to cook most of the Nigerian dishes and how to enjoy my time in the kitchen. I want to thank my friends – Yvette Richards who unknowingly taught me some Gambia dishes, Stella Oresusi, Kemi Adeeso, and Melissa Milligan who gave me suggestions for the book title. Without their encouragement and suggestions, I would not have been able to write this book in a timely manner. I would like to express my gratitude to my very dear friend - Lamide Odutola for all her encouraging and praise words, her willingness to try the recipes when I make them and for reading the first draft of the manuscript. I am greatly indebted to my sister Funke Ogunleye and my brother Gunju Olawole who gave me several suggestions for the Nigerian delicacies. Without their input this book would be sorely lacking our family recipe flavor.

Lastly, I thank my wonderful husband and friend, Abiodun Adegoke, for the love, care and support that he gave me during the writing of this manuscript. He who always refers to me as "the anointed fingers" was my mentor and encourager in putting everything together. Without his support and love, I would not be able to be the best that I can be as an author.

Lola Adegoke
October 2001
Email address: l_adegoke@yahoo.com

Contents

Introduction 13

Appetizers

Broiled Plantain (Boli) 17
Fried Plantain Pizza 18
Scotch Egg 19
Currant Loaves 20
Mozzarella, Tomato and Basil Bruschetta 21
Chin-Chin 22
Puff-Puff (Nigerian Dough Nut) 23
Hot & Spicy Beef Satay (Suya) 24

Soups
Traditional Chicken & Vegetable Soup 27
Minestrone Soup 28
Goat Pepper Soup 29
Guinea Hen Pepper Soup 30
Fish Pepper Soup 31
Oxtail Pepper Soup 32
Everything Pepper Soup 33
Low Calories Clam Chowder 34
Seafood Bisque 35
French Onion Soup 36
Tomato Soup 37

Salads
Very Fruity Salad 411
Italian Hand Tossed Salad 422
Mixed Greens Salad 43
Broccoli Salad 44
Spinach and Sun-Dried Tomato Pasta Salad 45
Tangy Coleslaw 46
Chicken Caesar-Cranberry Pasta Salad 47
Snow Peas and Chicken Vinaigrette Pasta Salad 48
Prawns and Artichoke Pasta Salad 49

Entrée
Fried Rice 53
Fried Yam & Pepper Dip (Dun-Dun & Ata) 54
Jollof Rice 55
Boiled Yam & Scrambled Eggs 57
Corned Beef Stew 58
Vegetable Lasagna 59
Everything Lasagna 60
Yam Pottage (Asaro) 61
Melon Stew (Egunsi) 62
Pesto Spaghetti with Meatballs 633
Spaghetti with Minced Meat 64
Steamed Bean Cakes (Moin-Moin) 65
Cowpea Fritters (Akara) 67
Yam Fritters (Ojojo) 68
Traditional Nigerian Bean Casserole (Ewa Riro) 69
Jerk Chicken 70
Tangy Chicken 71
Grilled Salmon Steak 72
Slow Cooking Meat Loaf 73
Slow Cooking Barbecue Steak 74
Slow Cooking Tasty Leg-of-Lamb 75
Tender and Spicy Baby Back Ribs 76
Honey and Garlic Ribs 77
Creamy Garlic Mashed Potato 78
Shepherd's Pie 79
Fisherman's Pie 80
Curry Goat 81
Curry Pork 82
Curry Prawn 833
Edikan-ikong 84
Ogbono 85
Yam Stew (Ikokore) 86

Deserts
Crème Brûlée Classic 89
Coffee – Brandy Crème Brûlée 90
Tiramisu' Classic 91
Signature Rum Carrot Cake 92
Moist Signature Banana Pound Cake 93
Sweet Honey Bun Cake 94
Heavenly Pound Cake 95

Lemony Pound Cake 96
Orange Pound Cake 97
Coconut Cake 98
Guinness Chocolate and Walnut Cake 100
Lift-Me-Up Chocolate Cake 101
Bread and Butter Pudding 102
Traditional Christmas Pudding 103
Christmas Cake 105
Apple Pie 106
Snacks 107
Sausage Rolls 109
Fish Rolls 110
Fish Cakes 111
Aussie Meat Pie 113
Nigerian Meat Pie 115
Steak and Kidney Pie 117
Sambusik (Lebanese Meat Patties) 118
Jamaican Patties 119
Mincemeat 121
Pita Bread 122
Sharwama 123
Breadfruit Fries 124

Non – Alcoholic Beverages
Summer PineLime Kisser 127
Coffee Punch Lift–Me-Up 128
Home-made Frappuccino 129
Cranberry Juice 130
Traditional Banana Milk Shake 131
Sweet Sensations 132
Hawaiian Exotic Fruit Punch 133
Warm Exotic and Spicy Autumn Punch 134
Creamy Orange 135
Absolute Lemonade 136
Berry Colada 137
Cappuccino Cooler 138
Honey and Fruit Smoothie 139

Seasonings and Spices 141

Conversion Chart 151

Introduction

Even though this book is in its first published edition, the book has existed in many forms prior to its publication. It has previously existed as recipe suggestions on Post-IT notes for friends that have tasted some of the menu included in this book. Many of the menus have been kept as a secret to bring our friends back to our house for more. This book is intended to reveal previously hidden menu secrets that friends and acquaintances have requested for. It is my hope that many will be able to expand their menu selections so that their creativity will become alive in the kitchen, which will increase the intimacy in their relationships with their spouses, children and dates.

The recipes ranges from authentic versions of some well known palates such as Tiramisu to unique and ethnic ones such as Jollof Rice. It is indeed from all parts of the world as it covers continents namely: Africa, Europe, Americas, Caribbean Islands, and the Middle East. The cookbook is aimed at promoting cultural awareness through food. It will convince readers on how to develop an international outlook and perspectives through food.
I have used a lot of fresh vegetables as opposed to canned ones in all recipes because the fresher they are, the more they impart the greatest flavor. As a time saving technique, try using prepared cut of meats such as cubed beef, pork, chicken, lamb or goat. For weight watchers, substitute skim milk where possible and use margarine instead of butter

In other to get the best out of this book, I will suggest that you share the food that you prepare with the recipe in this book, with your friends. When you share the food with your friends, and they cook another menu and invite you, together you will be able to sample many of the recipes with half the effort, if you had to prepare everything on your own. When you share the menu with friends, together you will become a blessing to each other and improve your friendship. Remember that it is more blessed to give than to receive. When you prepare the menu in this book and other ideas occurred to you that were not in this book, I will encourage you to write to us in other to enable us share that tip with the other readers. When you write us with such tips, it may be included in the second edition with reference to the reader that submitted it.

I hope and believe that, this book will make your kitchen come alive, and make cooking an enjoyable hobby rather than a dreaded chore for all. And lastly, may I suggest listening to your favorite artist while you cook, it takes away the boredom and replaces it with joy and calmness.

Appetizers

Broiled Plantain (Boli)

Plantain is a fruit of the Musa Paradisiaca, a type of banana plant. Plantains are more starchy than bananas but can be eaten uncooked. They are a staple crop in much of Africa, and are served boiled, steamed, baked, or fried. Boli to Nigerians is what Fish and Chips is to the English.

Ingredients:

- ❖ 2 ripe plantains, firm
- ❖ ¼ teaspoon salt (optional)
- ❖ 1 cup roasted peanuts

Cooking Instructions:

- ❖ Preheat the oven (broil) to 350F
- ❖ Peel the plantains, cut into two halves and rub salt on them
- ❖ Place the plantains under the broil for 5-10 minutes, until slightly brown
- ❖ Turn the plantains over to broil the under side
- ❖ The plantain color should turn yellow as it cooks
- ❖ Once the two sides are slightly brown, it is cooked
- ❖ Serve plantains hot with some roasted peanuts

Servings: 4
Per serving: 345 calories, 256 fat calories, 28.5g total fat, 4g saturated fat, 0mg cholesterol, 617mg sodium, 65.2g carbohydrate, 8.4g dietary fiber, 14.8g protein

Fried Plantain Pizza

Ingredients:

- ❖ 3 ripe plantains
- ❖ ¼ teaspoon salt (optional)
- ❖ 1 cup shredded five pizza Cheese (Kraft)

Cooking Instructions:

- ❖ Fill the deep fat fryer to min mark with oil and preheat to 350F
- ❖ Peel the plantains and slice diagonally (not lengthwise). A plantain should give about 10 or more slices
- ❖ Sprinkle salt on the sliced plantains
- ❖ Deep fry the plantain slices until golden brown
- ❖ Drain off the oil and turn plantain onto a platter
- ❖ Add the diced tomato and green pepper
- ❖ Top with the shredded cheese while plantain is still hot to melt it
- ❖ Serve hot as a side or as a meal

Servings: 6
Per serving: 236 calories, 68 fat calories, 7.5g total fat, 4.7g saturated fat, 23mg cholesterol, 240mg sodium, 35.7g carbohydrate, 2.6g dietary fiber, 6.4g protein

Scotch Egg

This snack originated from Scotland but it is a very popular finger food in Nigeria. In Scotland, it is also called Scots Eggs, and served as a savory. A great picnic favorite when served with a salad. Traditionally, Scotch Eggs are deep-fried but for a low calorie version, it can be baked in the oven at 375 F for about 20 minutes or until the sausage covering is firm when picked at with a knife or fork

Ingredients:

- ❖ 8 Eggs, hard cooked
- ❖ 1 egg, lightly whisked
- ❖ 2 lb. Sausage meat
- ❖ ½ cup bread crumbs
- ❖ 1/3 cup wholemeal flour
- ❖ freshly ground black pepper to taste
- ❖ ½ teaspoon salt

Cooking Instructions:

- ❖ Shell hard cooked eggs and rinse in cold water
- ❖ Mix some flour, salt, and pepper and sprinkle on a pastry board
- ❖ Divide the sausage into eight parts and flatten in a round shape on floured board
- ❖ Roll the eggs in the reserved flour
- ❖ Wrap each flattened sausage around the eggs to completely encase them and flatten the ends so that the eggs will stand upright
- ❖ Put some breadcrumbs on a piece of foil or in a foil pie dish
- ❖ Brush the coated eggs with the whisked egg and then roll them in the bread crumbs to cover
- ❖ Fill the deep fat fryer to max mark with oil and preheat to 300F
- ❖ Fry scotch eggs until brown on all sides and drain on paper towels
- ❖ Cut Scotch Eggs in half and serve hot or cold on a bed of lettuce

Servings: 4
Per serving: 443 calories, 284 fat calories, 31.6g total fat, 5.7g saturated fat, 238mg cholesterol, 1076mg sodium, 11.8g carbohydrate, 3.2g dietary fiber, 28g protein

Currant Loaves

Ingredients:

- ❖ ½ cup hot milk
- ❖ ½ cup hot water
- ❖ ½ cup bread crumbs
- ❖ 1 teaspoon granulated sugar
- ❖ ½ oz dried yeast
- ❖ 1 lb. wholemeal white flour
- ❖ 2 teaspoons salt
- ❖ 1 oz margarine
- ❖ 1 oz caster sugar
- ❖ 4 oz currants

Cooking Instructions:

- ❖ Dissolve 1 teaspoon sugar in a bowl of hot milk and water
- ❖ Stir in the yeast and leave in a warm place for 15 minutes or until frothy
- ❖ Add flour and salt in a large mixing bowl and rub in margarine
- ❖ Add sugar, yeast mixture and currants to the flour mixture
- ❖ Mix well together to form dough and knead thoroughly until no longer sticky
- ❖ Place dough in greased bowl and cover with greased film or place in greased ziploc bag
- ❖ Leave dough to rise, in warm place for 1 hour, until it is doubled in size
- ❖ Turn dough out onto lightly floured surface and knead for about 5 minutes
- ❖ Cut dough in half and shape each piece to fit greased loaf tins
- ❖ Place tins in large greased polythene bag
- ❖ Leave to rise until double in size
- ❖ Preheat oven to 375F and bake for 30-35 minutes
- ❖ Optionally glaze with icing sugar while hot and serve

Servings: 6
Per serving: 437 calories, 50 fat calories, 5.6g total fat, 1.1g saturated fat, 2mg cholesterol, 881mg sodium, 85.5g carbohydrate, 4g dietary fiber, 11.3g protein

Mozzarella, Tomato and Basil Bruschetta

Lots of Italian restaurants serve bruschetta as an 'Antipasto' or appetizer and it is great with drinks before lunch or dinner. An antipasto in Italy can be served hot or cold. One way to serve bruschetta is detailed below but another way is to mix all ingredients in a bowl and set bowl at table alongside the toasted bread and simply spoon on mixture. Traditionally, varied antipasto is set out at weddings, baptisms, first communion, birthdays, parties, or any special occasion.

Ingredients:

- ❖ Italian style country bread, sliced in ½ inch slices
- ❖ 2 medium fresh and ripe tomato, coarsely chopped
- ❖ 4 oz mozzarella cheese in small cubes
- ❖ 1 oz fresh basil leaves, shredded
- ❖ 3 tablespoons extra virgin olive oil
- ❖ garlic, peeled, whole (optional)
- ❖ salt to taste

Cooking Instructions:

- ❖ Toast bread slices over a charcoal grill
- ❖ Rub toast with a clove of garlic
- ❖ Drizzle with olive oil
- ❖ Spoon chopped tomato and cubed mozzarella onto bread
- ❖ Scatter some basil and salt to taste

Servings: 4
Per serving: 334 calories, 152 fat calories, 16.7g total fat, 4.6g saturated fat, 16mg cholesterol, 615mg sodium, 33.2g carbohydrate, 2.2g dietary fiber, 12.8g protein

Chin-Chin

This is a very tasty appetizer served during birthday parties and weddings in Nigeria

Ingredients:

- ❖ 6 cups self raising flour
- ❖ 1 lb. of butter
- ❖ 3 eggs
- ❖ 1 cup of water
- ❖ 1 cup of milk
- ❖ 1½ teaspoon baking powder
- ❖ 1 cup of granulated sugar

Cooking Instructions:

- ❖ Add all the ingredients together in a mixing bowl
- ❖ Mix and knead the dough until very smooth
- ❖ Roll the dough on a floured pastry board into half an inch thickness and sprinkle more flour on the dough if needed to prevent it from sticking
- ❖ Cut the dough into thin strips and then cut the strips into tiny slanted squares of ½ inch
- ❖ Sprinkle some flour on the pieces to prevent them from sticking together
- ❖ Fill the deep fat fryer to max mark with oil and preheat to 350F
- ❖ Fry the pieces in oil for 10–15 minutes until golden brown
- ❖ Allow oil to drain and serve on a platter. To garnish, sprinkle some confectionery sugar on it

Servings: 50
Per serving: 141 calories, 71 fat calories, 7.9g total fat, 4.8g saturated fat, 33mg cholesterol, 271mg sodium, 15.4g carbohydrate, 0.4g dietary fiber, 2.2g protein

Puff-Puff (Nigerian Dough Nut)

This appetizer is typically served during baby naming ceremonies, forty days after birth thanksgiving and wake keeping in Nigeria.

Ingredients:

- ❖ 2 cups wholemeal flour
- ❖ 2 cups water
- ❖ ½ cup sugar
- ❖ 1 teaspoon of cinnamon
- ❖ 2 teaspoon dry yeast

Cooking Instructions:

- ❖ Combine and mix the flour, sugar, water, and yeast together in a mixing bowl until the batter is smooth
- ❖ Leave the dough to rise for about 3 hours in a warm place
- ❖ Pre-heat oil in deep fat fryer to 350 F
- ❖ Using a large and deep soup spoon, drop a ball shaped dough into the oil
- ❖ Turn the frying dough over once the underneath is golden brown
- ❖ Line a bowl with kitchen towel and turn the golden brown puff-puff into the bowl to drain off excess oil
- ❖ Sprinkle with sugar and serve on a platter

Servings: 20
Per serving: 85 calories, 20 fat calories, 2.1g total fat, 0.3g saturated fat, 0mg cholesterol, 0mg sodium, 14.7g carbohydrate, 0.5g dietary fiber, 1.5g protein

Hot & Spicy Beef Satay (Suya)

This is my favorite everyday finger food. It is very hot and spicy therefore caution should be used when eating this. All foreigners are drawn to Suya once they get to Nigeria. Traditionally, it is a Northern Nigerian snack, grilled on an open bon fire by the Hausa tribe. People enjoy folk tales and drinks with Suya as an after work pastime. Varieties of Suya include chicken, fish and snail.

Ingredients:

- ❖ 2 lb. beef, cut into flat strips
- ❖ 1 cup Suya pepper
- ❖ ½ teaspoon salt
- ❖ 2 tablespoon Kuli-Kuli (finely ground roasted and fried peanuts)
- ❖ 2 medium tomatoes, sliced
- ❖ 2 medium sweet vidalia onions, sliced
- ❖ Wooden or metal skewers for grilling

Cooking Instructions:

- ❖ Mix the Suya pepper, salt and Kuli-Kuli together
- ❖ Coat the beef strips in the pepper mixture
- ❖ Arrange the beef strips on a wooden or metal skewer
- ❖ Brush strips with vegetable oil
- ❖ Grill on a barbecue grill or broil in the oven
- ❖ Turn from side to side frequently until done. Brush with more oil as needed
- ❖ Serve on a platter of lettuce and garnish with the tomato and onion slices

Servings: 4
Per serving: 743 calories, 352 fat calories, 38.5g total fat, 10.7g saturated fat, 173mg cholesterol, 478mg sodium, 26.4g carbohydrate, 12.8g dietary fiber, 71.4g protein

Soups

Traditional Chicken & Vegetable Soup

Ingredients:

- 1 onion
- 2 cloves garlic, minced
- 4 cups chicken broth
- 1 red bell pepper chopped
- 1 yellow bell pepper chopped
- ¼ teaspoon salt
- ½ teaspoon ground black pepper
- 2 tablespoon fresh parsley, chopped
- ¼ teaspoon dried thyme
- 2 tablespoon Olive oil
- ½ teaspoon ground white pepper
- 1½ lb. Boneless, skinless chicken breasts diced
- 1 cup sweet corn (fresh or frozen)
- 1 rib celery, chopped
- 1 small squash diced
- 1 small zucchini diced

Cooking Instructions:

- Add olive oil to a large saucepan and brown the chicken over medium heat
- Add the garlic and onion to the saucepan and cook for about 5 minutes
- Add the remaining ingredients except parsley and bring to a boil
- Let it simmer on low heat for 8 – 10 minutes
- Add the parsley and turn off the heat
- Serve hot with salad or as an appetizer

Servings: 6
Per serving: 235 calories, 59 fat calories, 6.5g total fat, 1.1g saturated fat, 65mg cholesterol, 712mg sodium, 15.1g carbohydrate, 2.4g dietary fiber, 29.1g protein

Minestrone Soup

Ingredients:

- ❖ 4 cups meat or vegetable broth
- ❖ ½ head of small cabbage, shredded
- ❖ 2 medium sized potatoes, peeled and chopped
- ❖ 1 small carrot, chopped
- ❖ 1 large leek, chopped
- ❖ 2 sticks celery, chopped
- ❖ 4 oz peas
- ❖ 4 oz green beans
- ❖ ½ clove garlic, finely chopped
- ❖ 2 medium tomatoes, peeled and sliced
- ❖ 1 oz bacon fat
- ❖ 1 oz rice

Cooking Instructions:

- ❖ Add the bacon fat to a saucepan, and sauté the garlic
- ❖ Add the vegetables except the tomatoes
- ❖ Stir fry for 10 mins without browning, stirring all the time
- ❖ Add the stock and bring to the boil
- ❖ Add the rice and sliced tomatoes
- ❖ Reduce heat to medium low and cook for 30-40 minutes
- ❖ Season with salt and pepper
- ❖ Serve hot

Servings: 6
Per serving: 117 calories, 19 fat calories, 2.2g total fat, 0.4g saturated fat, 0mg cholesterol, 610mg sodium, 18.5g carbohydrate, 3.7g dietary fiber, 6g protein

Goat Pepper Soup

This is the most popular soup and a favorite of beer and palm wine lovers in Nigeria. The Ibo tribe calls the soup Nwo-Nwo. It is mostly eaten in the evenings after a long day's work

Ingredients:

- ¼ cup canola oil
- 2 medium onions, quartered
- 3 lb. stew goat (with bones), cut into bite-sized pieces
- 3 hot chili peppers, diced
- 1 clove garlic, crushed
- 4 oz pepper soup seasoning
- salt (to taste)
- black pepper (to taste)
- 1 oz utazi leaves
- 1 oz mint leaves
- 2 cups water

Cooking Instructions:

- Add oil to a large saucepan or dutch oven
- Add the onions and stir fry for 3 minutes on medium high
- Add the meat, salt, garlic, chili and water and bring to a boil for 10 minutes
- Reduce heat to medium and cook meat for 10-15 minutes
- Add the pepper soup seasoning and let it simmer for 15-20 minutes or until meat is tender, stirring occasionally
- Add black pepper, mint and utazi leaves, stir and let it simmer for 10 minutes on medium low
- Serve hot in a soup bowl

Servings: 8
Per serving: 197 calories, 99 fat calories, 10.9g total fat, 1.3g saturated fat, 8mg cholesterol, 427mg sodium, 19.5g carbohydrate, 5.5g dietary fiber, 5.1g protein

Guinea Hen Pepper Soup

Guinea Fowl is a common name for six species of birds native to Africa. This bird has delicate, exquisite meat, considered by some to be superior to pheasant and it may be roasted, or cooked like a pheasant

Ingredients:

- ¼ cup canola oil
- 2 medium onions, quartered
- 3 lb. of guinea hen (with bones), cut into bite-sized pieces
- 3 hot chili peppers, diced
- 1 clove garlic, crushed
- 4 oz pepper soup seasoning
- salt (to taste)
- 1 chicken bouillon cube
- black pepper (to taste)
- 1 oz mint leaves
- 2 oz crayfish, ground
- 2 cups water

Cooking Instructions:

- Add oil to a large saucepan or dutch oven
- Add the onions and stir fry for 3 minutes on medium high
- Add the meat, salt, garlic, chili and water and bring to a boil for 10 minutes
- Reduce heat to medium and cook meat for 10-15 minutes
- Add the pepper soup seasoning and let it simmer for 15-20 minutes or until meat is tender, stirring occasionally
- Add black pepper, bouillon, crayfish and mint leaves, stir and let it simmer for 10 minutes on medium low
- Serve hot in a soup bowl

Servings: 8
Per serving: 318 calories, 111 fat calories, 12.3g total fat, 1.9g saturated fat, 116mg cholesterol, 434mg sodium, 14g carbohydrate, 3.9g dietary fiber, 37.8g protein

Fish Pepper Soup

Ingredients:

- ❖ 3 lb. of Catfish or Tilapia, cut into medium slices
- ❖ 4 oz fresh prawns
- ❖ 2 large lemon
- ❖ 1 teaspoon vinegar
- ❖ 1 teaspoon fish sauce
- ❖ 3 hot chili peppers, diced
- ❖ 4 oz pepper soup seasoning
- ❖ salt (to taste)
- ❖ ½ teaspoon black pepper
- ❖ 1 fish bouillon cube
- ❖ 1 oz mint leaves
- ❖ 3 cups water

Cooking Instructions:

- ❖ Wash fish with lemon and vinegar to remove the slime
- ❖ Season fish with salt and fish sauce, marinade for 30 minutes in the refrigerator
- ❖ Add seasoning, bouillon cube, chili and water in a large saucepan and bring to a boil for 10-15 minutes on medium high
- ❖ Add fish and prawns to mixture and cook for 20-25 minutes on medium
- ❖ Add black pepper and mint leaves, stir and let it simmer for 2 minutes on medium low
- ❖ Serve hot in a soup bowl

Servings: 8
Per serving: 235 calories, 57 fat calories, 6.2g total fat, 1.6g saturated fat, 120mg cholesterol, 407mg sodium, 12.4g carbohydrate, 3.5g dietary fiber, 3.2g protein

Oxtail Pepper Soup

Ingredients:

- ¼ cup canola oil
- 2 medium onions, quartered
- 3 lb. oxtail, cut into bite-sized chunks
- 3 hot chili peppers, ground
- 4 oz pepper soup seasoning
- 2 oz crayfish, ground
- 1 beef bouillon cube
- salt (to taste)
- black pepper (to taste)
- 1 oz utazi leaves
- 1 oz mint leaves
- 3 cups water

Cooking Instructions:

- Add oil to a large saucepan or dutch oven
- Add the onions and stir fry for 3 minutes on medium high
- Add oxtail, salt, bouillon, chili and water and bring to a boil for 20 minutes
- Reduce heat to medium and cook meat for 15-20 minutes
- Add the pepper soup seasoning and let it simmer for 15-20 minutes or until meat is tender, stirring occasionally
- Add black pepper, crayfish, mint and utazi leaves, stir and let it simmer for 10 minutes on medium low
- Serve hot in a soup bowl

Servings: 8
Per serving: 426 calories, 230 fat calories, 25.4g total fat, 8.3g saturated fat, 111mg cholesterol, 429mg sodium, 14g carbohydrate, 3.9g dietary fiber, 34.9g protein

Everything Pepper Soup

Ingredients:

- ¼ cup canola oil
- 2 medium onions, quartered
- 1 lb. oxtail, cut into bite-sized chunks
- ½ lb. tripe, bite size chunks
- ½ lb. cow foot, bite size chunks
- ½ lb. kidneys, bite size chunks
- ½ lb. beef ribs, bite size chunks
- 3 hot chili peppers, ground
- 4 oz pepper soup seasoning
- 2 oz crayfish, ground
- 1 beef bouillon cube
- salt (to taste)
- black pepper (to taste)
- 2 oz utazi leaves
- 2 oz mint leaves
- 4 cups water

Cooking Instructions:

- Rinse kidney in cold water and marinade in salty water for 45 minutes
- Strain the kidney and cook for 5 minutes on medium high
- Rinse kidney and set aside
- Add oil to a large saucepan or dutch oven
- Add the onions and stir fry for 3 minutes on medium high
- Add oxtail, tripe, ribs, cow foot, salt, bouillon, chili, water and bring to a boil for 40-45 minutes or until tender
- Reduce heat to medium and add kidney
- Add the pepper soup seasoning and let it simmer for 15-20 minutes
- Add black pepper, crayfish, mint and utazi leaves, stir and let it simmer for 10 minutes on medium low
- Serve hot in a soup bowl

Servings: 10
Per serving: 326 calories, 150 fat calories, 16.6g total fat, 4.7g saturated fat, 162mg cholesterol, 377mg sodium, 11.7g carbohydrate, 3.1g dietary fiber, 32.6g protein

Low Calories Clam Chowder

Ingredients:

- ❖ 2 medium onions, chopped
- ❖ 1 clove garlic, minced
- ❖ 1¾ cups water
- ❖ 4 small potatoes, peeled and diced
- ❖ 1 cup 2% fat milk
- ❖ ¼ teaspoon dried thyme
- ❖ 1 scallion, sliced
- ❖ 1 ½ cups clam juice
- ❖ 2 tablespoon reduced fat margarine
- ❖ 2 oz 99% fat free smoked ham, chopped
- ❖ 2 ½ doz. Clams, cleaned

Cooking Instructions:

- ❖ Add water to a large saucepan and bring to a boil then reduce heat to medium
- ❖ Add the clams and simmer covered until all clams open
- ❖ Remove clams from liquid into a bowl and discard shells
- ❖ Strain the clam broth through a strainer and set aside
- ❖ Add the margarine to the saucepan over medium heat
- ❖ Add the onions, ham, garlic, and potatoes to the melted margarine
- ❖ Cook for 5 minutes, stirring occasionally
- ❖ Add the broth, clam juice, and thyme and bring to a boil over medium heat
- ❖ Reduce heat and simmer covered for 15-20 minutes
- ❖ Allow the mixture to cool down slightly
- ❖ Puree half of mixture in a food processor and return to saucepan
- ❖ Stir in the milk and bring to a simmer
- ❖ Stir in the clams and garnish with scallions
- ❖ Serve hot

Servings: 6
Per serving: 179 calories, 53 fat calories, 5.9g total fat, 1.4g saturated fat, 35mg cholesterol, 315mg sodium, 17.1g carbohydrate, 1.7g dietary fiber, 14.5g protein

Seafood Bisque

Ingredients:

- ❖ 1 onion, finely chopped
- ❖ 3½ cups vegetable broth
- ❖ 2 plum tomatoes, diced
- ❖ 1½ cups milk
- ❖ 1 teaspoon paprika
- ❖ 2 tablespoon reduced fat margarine
- ❖ ½ cup hunts tomato puree (oregano, basil, garlic)
- ❖ 1 tablespoon chopped fresh parsley
- ❖ ½ cup dry white wine
- ❖ ¼ teaspoon salt
- ❖ ½ lb. shelled lobster tail, diced
- ❖ ½ lb. king prawns, diced
- ❖ ½ lb. crab meat
- ❖ ¼ teaspoon hot pepper sauce
- ❖ ½ teaspoon ground white pepper
- ❖ 2 ¼ tablespoon all purpose flour

Cooking Instructions:

- ❖ Add the margarine to the saucepan over medium-high heat
- ❖ Add the onion to the melted margarine and cook stirring for 5 minutes
- ❖ Stir in the flour and cook stirring for until lightly browned
- ❖ Add the broth, tomato puree, wine, and salt. Bring to a boil over medium heat
- ❖ Reduce heat to low and simmer, covered for 10 minutes
- ❖ Add the prawns, lobster, and crabmeat
- ❖ Cover and simmer for 5-7minutes until lobster and prawns are opaque
- ❖ Stir in the milk, hot pepper sauce, and paprika
- ❖ Cook on medium heat for 4 minutes
- ❖ Stir in the plum tomatoes and parsley
- ❖ Serve hot

Servings: 4
Per serving: 248 calories, 72 fat calories, 8.1g total fat, 1.7g saturated fat, 184mg cholesterol, 587mg sodium, 10g carbohydrate, 1.6g dietary fiber, 34g protein

French Onion Soup

Ingredients:

- ❖ 8 large sweet onions, thinly sliced into rings
- ❖ 4 cups beef broth
- ❖ ½ teaspoon freshly ground black pepper
- ❖ ¼ cup fresh parsley, chopped
- ❖ 2 tablespoon olive oil
- ❖ ½ teaspoon ground white pepper
- ❖ ½ cup shredded smoked Gouda cheese
- ❖ 4 slices French bread, lightly toasted
- ❖ 2 tablespoon all-purpose flour
- ❖ mild pepper sauce
- ❖ 2 cups water

Cooking Instructions:

- ❖ Heat olive oil in a large saucepan over medium heat
- ❖ Add the onions to the saucepan and cook stirring for about 5 minutes
- ❖ Reduce heat to low and cook covered for 10 minutes until very soft
- ❖ Remove pan cover and increase heat to medium
- ❖ Cook stirring frequently for 25-30 minutes until onions are golden
- ❖ Add the ground pepper and flour over the onions and stir
- ❖ Add the broth and water stirring well to smooth out the lumps
- ❖ Bring to a boil, reduce the heat to low, cover and simmer for 25 minutes
- ❖ Stir in the mild pepper sauce
- ❖ Preheat the oven to 425F
- ❖ Ladle the soup into 4 soup bowls, top each with the bread, cheese and parsley
- ❖ Bake for 5-6 minutes until cheese is melted and bubbly

Servings: 4
Per serving: 346 calories, 146 fat calories, 16.2g total fat, 6.6g saturated fat, 32mg cholesterol, 1200mg sodium, 34.9g carbohydrate, 4.4g dietary fiber, 15g protein

Tomato Soup

Ingredients:

- ❖ 1 small onion, chopped
- ❖ 2 cups beef broth
- ❖ 1 tablespoon olive oil
- ❖ 1 teaspoon dried basil, crushed
- ❖ 14 oz can diced tomatoes (oregano, garlic, basil)
- ❖ ¼ cup milk
- ❖ ¼ teaspoon freshly ground black pepper

Cooking Instructions:

- ❖ Heat olive oil in a large saucepan over medium heat
- ❖ Add the onions to the saucepan and cook stirring for about 5 minutes
- ❖ Add the broth, tomatoes, basil and bring to a boil
- ❖ Remove pan cover and increase heat to medium
- ❖ Reduce the heat to low, cover and simmer for 15-20 minutes until slightly thickened
- ❖ Allow to cool for 10 minutes
- ❖ Puree mixture in a food processor and return to saucepan
- ❖ Add milk and cook until heated through
- ❖ Season with pepper
- ❖ Serve hot

Servings: 4
Per serving: 91 calories, 38 fat calories, 4.3g total fat, 1g saturated fat, 1mg cholesterol, 530mg sodium, 9.4g carbohydrate, 2.5g dietary fiber, 3.8g protein

Salads

Very Fruity Salad

Ingredients:

- ❖ 1 apple (peeled, cored and chopped)
- ❖ 1 Granny Smith apple (peeled, cored and chopped)
- ❖ 1 nectarine, pitted and sliced
- ❖ 2 stalks celery, chopped
- ❖ ½ cup dried cranberries
- ❖ ½ cup chopped walnuts
- ❖ 1 (8 oz) container nonfat lemon yogurt
- ❖ 1 cup red seedless grapes (halved)

Cooking Instructions:

- ❖ Wash and drain fruits on a paper towel
- ❖ In a large bowl, combine apples, nectarine, celery, and walnuts
- ❖ Mix in yogurt and chill until ready to serve
- ❖ Just before serving, add the cranberries and toss well
- ❖ Serve in a fruit salad bowl

Servings: 6
Per serving: 171 calories, 62 fat calories, 7g total fat, 0g saturated fat, 0mg cholesterol, 37mg sodium, 25g carbohydrate, 3g dietary fiber, 4g protein

Italian Hand Tossed Salad

Ingredients:

- ❖ 6 oz young spinach
- ❖ ¼ teaspoon salt
- ❖ ¼ teaspoon freshly ground black pepper
- ❖ ¼ teaspoon ground white pepper
- ❖ 3 oz fresh mozzarella cheese, diced
- ❖ 4 oz cherry tomatoes, halved
- ❖ 2 tablespoon Italian dressing
- ❖ 2 oz dried cranberries

Cooking Instructions:

- ❖ Wash and drain spinach on a paper towel
- ❖ Place spinach in a salad bowl
- ❖ Add the mozzarella cheese and cherry tomatoes
- ❖ Toss the mixture
- ❖ Sprinkle the Italian dressing on the salad
- ❖ Add salt and pepper to taste
- ❖ Add the dried cranberries
- ❖ Serve with home made garlic bread

Servings: 4
Per serving: 158 calories, 67 fat calories, 7.1g total fat, 2.7g saturated fat, 12mg cholesterol, 337mg sodium, 15.5g carbohydrate, 2.1g dietary fiber, 7.3g protein

Mixed Greens Salad

Ingredients:

- ❖ 1 head Bibb lettuce
- ❖ ½ head escarole
- ❖ 1 small bunch arugula
- ❖ ½ head romaine
- ❖ 1 small bunch field lettuce
- ❖ ½ head curly chicory
- ❖ Coarse salt
- ❖ 2 tablespoons fresh lemon juice
- ❖ 6 tablespoons extra virgin olive oil
- ❖ Freshly ground black pepper

Cooking Instructions:

- ❖ Wash the greens thoroughly until free of all dirt and dry completely
- ❖ Place greens in a plastic bag and refrigerate until needed
- ❖ Add a teaspoon of salt in a small bowl and add lemon juice, stir to dissolve salt
- ❖ Add the olive oil and pepper to taste, mix well
- ❖ Tear the greens into bite-size pieces with your hands
- ❖ Pour the dressing over the greens, tossing until the greens are well coated
- ❖ Serve salad immediately

Servings: 8
Per serving: 119 calories, 95 fat calories, 10.5g total fat, 1.4g saturated fat, 0mg cholesterol, 163mg sodium, 4g carbohydrate, 2g dietary fiber, 1.9g protein

Broccoli Salad

Ingredients:

- 10 slices bacon
- 1 head fresh broccoli (cut into bite size pieces)
- ¼ cup sweet onion, chopped
- ½ cup raisins
- 3 tablespoons white wine vinegar
- 2 tablespoons white sugar
- 1 cup mayonnaise
- 1 cup sunflower seeds

Cooking Instructions:

- Cook bacon in a large, deep skillet over medium high heat until evenly brown
- Drain bacon on a kitchen towel, crumble and set aside
- Combine the broccoli, onion and raisins in a medium bowl
- Whisk together the vinegar, sugar and mayonnaise
- Pour over broccoli mixture, and toss until well mixed
- Refrigerate for at least two hours
- Just before serving, toss salad with crumbled bacon and sunflower seeds
- Serve salad as a main meal or an appetizer

Servings: 6
Per serving: 746 calories, 636 fat calories, 71g total fat, 16g saturated fat, 51mg cholesterol, 584mg sodium, 21g carbohydrate, 5g dietary fiber, 12g protein

Spinach and Sun-Dried Tomato Pasta Salad

Ingredients:

- ❖ 15 sun-dried tomatoes, cut in thin strips
- ❖ 4 scallions, sliced in rounds
- ❖ 1 lb. fresh baby spinach, washed and well drained
- ❖ 3 anchovy fillets, drained and chopped
- ❖ ½ cup walnuts, lightly toasted and coarsely chopped
- ❖ 4 tablespoons extra virgin olive oil
- ❖ cayenne pepper to taste
- ❖ salt and freshly ground black pepper
- ❖ 1 lb. pasta shells or bows

Cooking Instructions:

- ❖ Cook pasta in a large steamer according to instruction on box
- ❖ Rinse in cold water and drain in a colander
- ❖ Toast the walnuts in a small heavy pan over medium heat for 5 minutes stirring
- ❖ Place pasta and tomato strips in a large serving bowl
- ❖ Add 2 tablespoons olive oil and toss
- ❖ Add scallions, spinach, anchovy, cayenne pepper, the rest of the olive oil to pasta
- ❖ Season with salt and pepper and toss
- ❖ Refrigerate for an hour or more
- ❖ Sprinkle walnuts on pasta and serve at room temperature

Servings: 8
Per serving: 215 calories, 57 fat calories, 6.1g total fat, 0.6g saturated fat, 4mg cholesterol, 796mg sodium, 29.7g carbohydrate, 5.8g dietary fiber, 9.9g protein

Tangy Coleslaw

As a college student in the UK, this coleslaw was my special treat on Sundays. The lemon juice and season-all gives it the tangy taste. I enjoy serving this with steamed rice and tangy chicken

Ingredients:

- ❖ 1 head firm white cabbage
- ❖ 4 medium carrots
- ❖ 1 oz dried cranberries
- ❖ ¼ teaspoon freshly ground black pepper
- ❖ ¼ teaspoon ground white pepper
- ❖ ¼ teaspoon season-all (Shwartz brand)
- ❖ 1 cup mayonnaise
- ❖ 1 large lemon

Cooking Instructions:

- ❖ Cut cabbage into two halves and shred
- ❖ Wash cabbage, drain and place in a mixing bowl
- ❖ Peel carrot, coarsely grate and add to mixing bowl
- ❖ Add the salt and pepper to the mayonnaise
- ❖ Add the mayonnaise to the mixing bowl
- ❖ Sprinkle season-all on the mixture
- ❖ Cut lemon in half and squeeze juice on mixture
- ❖ Toss to mix well
- ❖ Place the coleslaw in the refrigerator to chill
- ❖ Sprinkle the cranberries on slaw just before serving

Servings: 10
Per serving: 149 calories, 74 fat calories, 8g total fat, 1.2g saturated fat, 6mg cholesterol, 188mg sodium, 16.9g carbohydrate, 2.8g dietary fiber, 1.9g protein

Chicken Caesar-Cranberry Pasta Salad

Ingredients:

- ❖ 16 oz Pasta Bows
- ❖ ¼ teaspoon salt
- ❖ ¼ teaspoon freshly ground black pepper
- ❖ ¼ teaspoon ground white pepper
- ❖ 2 cups chopped grilled chicken
- ❖ ¼ cup fresh parsley, chopped
- ❖ ¾ cup shaved parmesan cheese
- ❖ 2 oz black olives, halved
- ❖ 3 tablespoons Caesar dressing (Ken's Caesar Lite)
- ❖ 3 oz dried cranberries

Cooking Instructions:

- ❖ Cook pasta in a large steamer according to instruction on box
- ❖ Rinse in cold water and drain in a colander
- ❖ Add pasta, chicken, cranberries and olives in a large salad bowl
- ❖ Toss the mixture
- ❖ Add salt and pepper to taste
- ❖ Add the Italian dressing on the salad and toss
- ❖ Sprinkle cheese and parsley on salad
- ❖ Serve immediately or chill in the refrigerator

Servings: 6
Per serving: 294 calories, 66 fat calories, 7.4g total fat, 3.1g saturated fat, 46mg cholesterol, 509mg sodium, 35.6g carbohydrate, 4.6g dietary fiber, 21.4g protein

Snow Peas and Chicken Vinaigrette Pasta Salad

Ingredients:

- ❖ 1 cup tender, fresh snow peas, washed and lightly steamed
- ❖ 1 cup fresh bean sprouts
- ❖ 1 cup cooked chicken breast
- ❖ 20 pitted green olives, chopped
- ❖ 2 tablespoons fresh lemon juice
- ❖ 6 tablespoons extra virgin olive oil
- ❖ 1 teaspoon mustard (optional)
- ❖ 1 clove of garlic, peeled and finely minced (optional)
- ❖ 1 teaspoon fresh ginger, minced (optional)
- ❖ salt and freshly ground black pepper to taste
- ❖ 8 oz cooked linguine or pasta of your choice

Cooking Instructions:

- ❖ Cook pasta in a large steamer according to instruction on box
- ❖ Rinse in cold water and drain in a colander
- ❖ Cut the chicken breasts into bite sized pieces
- ❖ Add lemon juice, mustard, garlic, ginger, salt and pepper in a mixing jar stirring.
- ❖ Add the olive oil and mix very well
- ❖ Combine the pasta and the rest of the ingredients in a large serving bowl, mixing
- ❖ Add the vinaigrette and stir
- ❖ Serve at room temperature or chill in the refrigerator

Servings: 4
Per serving: 504 calories, 214 fat calories, 23.9g total fat, 3g saturated fat, 33mg cholesterol, 467mg sodium, 49.7g carbohydrate, 3.7g dietary fiber, 22.7g protein

Prawns and Artichoke Pasta Salad

Ingredients:

- ❖ ½ lb. medium shells or farfalle pasta
- ❖ 1 (9 oz) package frozen artichoke hearts
- ❖ Salt and freshly ground black pepper
- ❖ 1 lb. frozen prawns, cooked
- ❖ ¼ teaspoon oregano leaves, dried
- ❖ 1 medium garlic, peeled and finely chopped
- ❖ 3 tablespoons extra virgin olive oil
- ❖ 1 tablespoons red wine vinegar

Cooking Instructions:

- ❖ Defrost prawns, drain in a colander and place on paper towels
- ❖ Defrost and steam artichoke hearts. Drain well and place on paper towels
- ❖ Rinse off with cold water and drain in a colander
- ❖ Add prawns and artichokes in large serving bowl, drizzle with olive oil and toss
- ❖ Cook pasta according to instruction on package, drain in a colander
- ❖ Add pasta to prawns and artichokes
- ❖ Add the rest of the olive oil, vinegar, garlic, oregano, salt and black pepper
- ❖ Mix well, cover with cling film and refrigerate for 4 hours or for a day
- ❖ Toss, add some more black pepper, garnish with oregano leaves and serve

Servings: 4
Per serving: 453 calories, 119 fat calories, 13.1g total fat, 1.7g saturated fat, 170mg cholesterol, 525mg sodium, 51g carbohydrate, 4.6g dietary fiber, 32.4g protein

Entrée

Fried Rice

Ingredients:

- 3½ cups of Uncle Ben's long grain rice
- 4 cups of hot water
- 1 large white / yellow onion (sliced in rings)
- 2 tablespoon margarine/butter
- ½ cup canola or olive oil
- 2 lb. large cooked shrimps, tail off
- 2 skinless chicken breasts (baked with season all), cut into cubes
- 1 cup broth from baked chicken
- 4 cups of mixed vegetables (carrots, sweet peas, corn, green beans)
- ½ teaspoon thyme
- 3 tablespoon authentic curry powder
- 4 chicken bullion cubes
- Salt to taste

Cooking Instructions:

- Wash the rice in warm water, and drain in a colander for 5 minutes
- In a large saucepan, add the oil and butter and heat on medium until butter melts
- Add the rice, onion, thyme, bouillon cubes, curry and season all
- Stir fry the rice for 5-10 minutes on high until slightly crispy but not burnt
- Add hot water to the rice and salt to taste, stirring
- Bring to a boil, cover and let it simmer on medium high for 10-15 minutes
- Check occasionally for enough water and rice tenderness, add more water as required
- Preheat oven to 350F
- Remove the lid and cover saucepan with foil
- Bake for 10-15minutes
- Add shrimps and mixed vegetables, fluffing the rice. Cover with foil and return to the oven for 5-10 minutes.
- Remove from the oven, stir in cubed chicken and turn into a serving dish.

Servings: 8
Per serving: 551 calories, 231 fat calories, 25.8g total fat, 4.1g saturated fat, 331mg cholesterol, 753mg sodium, 30.3g carbohydrate, 5.1g dietary fiber, 49.7g protein

Fried Yam & Pepper Dip
(Dun-Dun & Ata)

Yams (Dioscorea batatas, and other species of Dioscorea) are common throughout the world's tropical areas. It is a staple diet in Nigeria and Africa as a whole. It is commonly used in Nigeria to make pounded yam (iyan) and yam flour (elubo)

Ingredients:

- ❖ 1 medium yam
- ❖ ¼ teaspoon salt
- ❖ 1 bell pepper
- ❖ 2 large tomato
- ❖ 1 teaspoon chili powder
- ❖ ¼ teaspoon season all
- ❖ ¼ teaspoon thyme
- ❖ ¼ teaspoon basil
- ❖ 2 medium onions, sliced
- ❖ 1 cup olive oil
- ❖ 1 beef bullion cube
- ❖ ½ cup hot water

Cooking Instructions:

- ❖ Peel the yam, cut into 2 inch wedges, rinse and soak in salty water for 30 minutes
- ❖ Drain yam in a colander, pat dry with a kitchen towel and add season all
- ❖ Fill the deep fat fryer to max mark with oil and preheat to 350F
- ❖ Fry yam until slightly brown
- ❖ Drain the yam of excess oil and turn into a serving dish
- ❖ To make the pepper dip, blend the peppers, tomato, and 1 onion in a blender
- ❖ Add olive oil, onions, water, salt, thyme, basil and the blended pepper in a skillet
- ❖ Cook on medium heat for 5-10 minutes, stirring occasionally
- ❖ Cover and cook on medium low for 15 minutes or until the dip is almost crispy looking
- ❖ Serve the pepper in a dip bowl

Servings: 4
Per serving: 812 calories, 494 fat calories, 54.8g total fat, 7.4g saturated fat, 0mg cholesterol, 188mg sodium, 74.3g carbohydrate, 11.7g dietary fiber, 5.2g protein

Jollof Rice

Jollof Rice is a very popular Nigerian dish served during special occasions like weddings, engagements, naming ceremonies, to name a few. It has its origins from the Wolof people of Senegal and Gambia who have a staple diet of rice and fish dish they call Ceebu Jen

Ingredients:

- 3 cups of Uncle Ben's long grain rice
- 4 cups of water
- 1 cup sherry cooking wine
- salt to taste
- 3 tablespoon of butter
- ¼ cup canola or olive oil
- 3 cups mixed vegetables
- ½ teaspoon curry powder
- 1 8oz can tomato puree (I use the Italian Herb variety by Hunt)
- 1 large red bell pepper, chopped
- 1 large sweet white/yellow onion, chopped
- 2 lbs. cooked shrimp, tail off
- 1 teaspoon habanero pepper or chili powder
- 1 large fresh tomato, chopped
- ¼ teaspoon thyme
- 4 dried whole bay leaves
- 2 chicken bullion cubes

Cooking Instructions:

- Wash the rice in warm water and drain in a colander
- Add water, sherry, oil and butter in a large saucepan, heat on medium high until butter melts
- Add the tomato puree, chili powder, thyme, curry powder, bay leaves and tomato
- Add the rice, chicken cubes and salt to taste
- Cover and let it simmer on medium heat for 15-20 minutes
- Check occasionally for enough water and rice tenderness
- Preheat oven to 350F

- ❖ Remove the lid; add onions and red bell pepper stirring. Cover saucepan with foil, make two slits in the foil and transfer to the oven and bake for 10-15 minutes
- ❖ Add cooked shrimps and mixed vegetables fluffing the rice. Cover with foil and return to the oven for 5 minutes.
- ❖ Remove the bay leaves and turn into a serving dish.

Servings: 8
Per serving: 634 calories, 230 fat calories, 25.4g total fat, 4.1g saturated fat, 443mg cholesterol, 1193mg sodium, 47g carbohydrate, 6.9g dietary fiber, 54g protein

Boiled Yam & Scrambled Eggs

Ingredients:

- ❖ 1 medium white or yellow yam
- ❖ 1 teaspoon salt
- ❖ 3 cups water
- ❖ 5 eggs
- ❖ 1 can sardine in tomato (hot & spicy)
- ❖ 2 tablespoons 2% low fat milk
- ❖ 1 cup frozen sweet pepper
- ❖ ¾ cup olive oil

Cooking Instructions:

- ❖ Cut yam into an inch slices and peel the yam, rinse in cold water
- ❖ Add 2 cups of water and the yam in a saucepan
- ❖ Add ½ teaspoon of salt
- ❖ Cook on medium high for 25-35 minutes or until soft
- ❖ Beat eggs in a bowl, add salt and milk to it and whisk
- ❖ Heat olive oil in a large skillet on medium
- ❖ Add sweet peppers and sardine to oil
- ❖ Cook on medium high stirring for 5 minutes
- ❖ Add eggs to the skillet and stir through for 3-5 minutes
- ❖ Serve yam hot on a flat plate with the scrambled egg on top

Servings: 6
Per serving: 439 calories, 247 fat calories, 27.5g total fat, 3.8g saturated fat, 3mg cholesterol, 446mg sodium, 43g carbohydrate, 6.4g dietary fiber, 5.1g protein

Corned Beef Stew

Ingredients:

- ❖ 1 can corned beef
- ❖ 1/8 teaspoon salt (optional)
- ❖ ¼ cup olive oil
- ❖ 1 medium onion, sliced
- ❖ ½ cup water
- ❖ ¼ teaspoon thyme
- ❖ 1 small tomato, diced
- ❖ 1 teaspoon chili powder
- ❖ ½ cup tomato sauce

Cooking Instructions:

- ❖ Add olive oil in a large saucepan and heat for 2 minutes on medium high
- ❖ Add onions, chili powder, tomato, tomato sauce and water
- ❖ Cook, stirring occasionally for 5 minutes on medium
- ❖ Add corned beef and stir through
- ❖ Add thyme and salt to taste (remember corned beef is salty)
- ❖ Add water and reduce heat to medium low
- ❖ Let it simmer for 5-10 minutes
- ❖ Serve over boiled yam

Servings: 6
Per serving: 188 calories, 132 fat calories, 14.6g total fat, 3.5g saturated fat, 32mg cholesterol, 506mg sodium, 3.3g carbohydrate, 0.7g dietary fiber, 10.7g protein

Vegetable Lasagna

Ingredients:

- ❖ 9 Lasagna sheets
- ❖ 1 lb. firm tofu
- ❖ 3 tablespoons nutritional yeast
- ❖ 1 lb. mushrooms, sliced
- ❖ 1 jar of Marinara sauce
- ❖ 1 bunch spinach or chard
- ❖ 1 teaspoon basil
- ❖ 1 teaspoon thyme
- ❖ 1 teaspoon freshly ground black pepper
- ❖ 1 onion, finely chopped
- ❖ 1½ cup cauliflower, chopped
- ❖ 3 tablespoons olive oil
- ❖ ½ teaspoon salt

Cooking Instructions:

- ❖ Mash the tofu in a bowl, add salt, yeast, spices, and ½ cup marinara sauce
- ❖ Sauté cauliflower and onion in oil for 5 minutes
- ❖ Add mushroom slices and continue to sauté for 2 minutes
- ❖ Add to tofu and mix well
- ❖ Oil a lasagna dish with olive oil
- ❖ Spread some of the Marinara sauce in the dish
- ❖ Arrange 3 of the lasagna sheets on the sauce
- ❖ Top the lasagna sheets with a layer of tofu and sautéed vegetables
- ❖ Wash and remove stem from spinach and sauté in water for 3 minutes
- ❖ Spread half evenly on the lasagna, and add more marinara sauce
- ❖ Repeat with noodles, tofu mixture, spinach and sauce
- ❖ For the top portion, layer noodles, remaining tofu and sauce
- ❖ Cover loosely with aluminum foil paper
- ❖ Preheat the oven to 375F
- ❖ Bake for 30mins
- ❖ Remove foil and bake for 5 mins
- ❖ Let cool on a rack, cut and serve with tossed salad

Servings: 8
Per serving: 352 calories, 122 fat calories, 13.5g total fat, 3.2g saturated fat, 9mg cholesterol, 756mg sodium, 38.9g carbohydrate, 5.6g dietary fiber, 18.5g protein

Everything Lasagna

Ingredients:

- ❖ 9 Lasagna sheets
- ❖ ¼ lb. zucchini slices
- ❖ 12 oz low fat ricotta cheese
- ❖ 8 oz shredded parmesan cheese
- ❖ 1 cup shredded low fat mozzarella cheese
- ❖ 1 jar of Marinara Sauce
- ❖ 56g Italian sausage slices
- ❖ 56g honey smoked turkey slices
- ❖ 56g Canadian Bacon slices

Cooking Instructions:

- ❖ Oil a lasagna dish with olive or canola oil
- ❖ Spread some of the Marinara sauce in the dish
- ❖ Arrange 3 of the lasagna sheets on the sauce
- ❖ Mix the ½ parmesan with ricotta cheese in a bowl
- ❖ Top the lasagna sheets with the zucchini and some of the bacon slices
- ❖ Add some of the cheese mixture, then Marinara sauce
- ❖ Add another layer of lasagna sheets and top with the fillings alternating
- ❖ After the last sets of lasagna sheets are added, spread the remaining Marinara sauce.
- ❖ Finally top with the remaining parmesan cheese and shredded mozzarella
- ❖ Cover loosely with aluminum foil paper
- ❖ Preheat the oven to 375F
- ❖ Put the lasagna in the oven and bake for 40mins or until cheese starts bubbling
- ❖ Remove foil and bake for 5 mins
- ❖ Let cool on a rack, cut and serve with tossed salad

Servings: 8
Per serving: 367 calories, 147 fat calories, 16.4g total fat, 8.4g saturated fat, 49mg cholesterol, 1150mg sodium, 31.9g carbohydrate, 4.3g dietary fiber, 23g protein

Yam Pottage (Asaro)

Ingredients:

- ❖ 1 medium white or yellow yam (Ghana/Nigeria)
- ❖ 2 sweet potato
- ❖ 4 tablespoon of palm oil
- ❖ 1 teaspoon salt to taste
- ❖ ¼ teaspoon thyme
- ❖ 2 chicken bullion cubes
- ❖ ¼ cup olive or canola oil
- ❖ 1 sweet red pepper
- ❖ 1 large tomato
- ❖ 1 medium onion
- ❖ Honey smoked turkey neck
- ❖ 2½ cups water

Cooking Instructions:

- ❖ Peel the yam and sweet potato, cut into cubes and rinse in cold water
- ❖ Add 2 cups of water, the yam and potato cubes in a large saucepan
- ❖ Add thyme and salt to taste
- ❖ Cook on medium high for 15-20 minutes
- ❖ Grind the peppers, onion and tomato in a blender or food processor
- ❖ Add some oil, palm oil and the ground pepper in a skillet, cook on medium low for 20 minutes
- ❖ Add the bouillon cubes, smoked turkey necks, 3 tablespoons of warm water to the sauce and cook for 5-10 minutes stirring occasionally
- ❖ Check the yam with a fork, if it breaks apart easily, it's cooked
- ❖ Add the sauce to the yam and stir with a wooden spoon, mashing 75% of the yam and potato in the process
- ❖ Cover and let it simmer for about 5 minutes
- ❖ Turn into a serving dish and garnish with thyme sprigs

Servings: 8
Per serving: 493 calories, 162 fat calories, 17.9g total fat, 5.7g saturated fat, 69mg cholesterol, 341mg sodium, 63.6g carbohydrate, 8.2g dietary fiber, 19.1g protein

Melon Stew (Egunsi)

The soup is made with ground seeds of a species of Cucurbitaceae, which includes melons, pumpkins, and squashes, many of which are native to Africa

Ingredients:

- ❖ 1½ cup Egunsi seeds, ground
- ❖ ¼ cup palm oil
- ❖ ½ teaspoon salt
- ❖ 2 beef bullion cubes
- ❖ 1 small smoked tilapia fish
- ❖ 1 small smoked cat fish
- ❖ 1 cup smoked prawns
- ❖ 1 tablespoon locust beans
- ❖ 1 lb. smoked cow skin or cooked tripe or oxtail or smoked turkey necks
- ❖ 2 cups fresh or dry bitter leaves/spinach/waterleaf/Ugwo chopped
- ❖ 1 red bell pepper, 1 tomato, 1 onion (grind in a blender)
- ❖ 1 tablespoon chili powder
- ❖ 4 oz crayfish
- ❖ 1 cup water

Cooking Instructions:

- ❖ Add the palm oil, chili powder and the blended pepper in a large saucepan
- ❖ Cook on medium high for about 5 minutes
- ❖ Add water, locust beans, prawns, fish, thyme, salt and smoked meat to the sauce
- ❖ Cover and cook for 10-15 minutes on medium until the meat is tender
- ❖ Add the ground melon and stir very well to avoid lumps
- ❖ Cover the pan and let it simmer for another 5-10 mins, stirring occasionally
- ❖ Add the bitter leaves and stir, mixing thoroughly.
- ❖ Cover and let it cook for another 5-10 mins
- ❖ Turn into a stew dish and serve with pounded yam, eba or fufu

Servings: 10
Per serving: 354 calories, 185 fat calories, 20.7g total fat, 6.2g saturated fat, 140mg cholesterol, 279mg sodium, 8g carbohydrate, 2.8g dietary fiber, 34.2g protein

Pesto Spaghetti with Meatballs

Ingredients:

- ❖ 1 packet of spaghettini nodules
- ❖ 1 lb. of spicy Italian meatballs
- ❖ 2 cups Marinara sauce
- ❖ 1 cup frozen sweet peppers
- ❖ 1 teaspoon salt
- ❖ ¼ teaspoon thyme
- ❖ 1 teaspoon chili powder
- ❖ ¼ cup olive oil
- ❖ 2 teaspoons Pesto
- ❖ 3 cups water

Cooking Instructions:

- ❖ Add some water, salt and olive oil in a steamer and bring to a boil
- ❖ Add the spaghettini nodules, water must cover nodules
- ❖ Cook uncovered for about 10 mins on high heat and drain
- ❖ Add the Pesto to the cooked spaghetti and toss
- ❖ Add the remaining olive oil, peppers, and the meatballs in a skillet and stir fry for 10 mins
- ❖ Add the Marinara sauce, chili powder and thyme and let it simmer for 5 minutes
- ❖ Serve spaghetti hot in a pasta bowl with the sauce on top

Servings: 4
Per serving: 958 calories, 335 fat calories, 37.9g total fat, 10.3g saturated fat, 115mg cholesterol, 830mg sodium, 104.1g carbohydrate, 8.1g dietary fiber, 51.7g protein

Spaghetti with Minced Meat

Ingredients:

* ❖ 1 packet of spaghettini nodules
* ❖ 1 lb. of minced meat
* ❖ 2 cups Marinara sauce
* ❖ 1 cup frozen sweet peppers
* ❖ 1 cup frozen mixed vegetables
* ❖ 1 large sweet vidalia onion, sliced
* ❖ 1 teaspoon salt
* ❖ ¼ teaspoon thyme
* ❖ 1 teaspoon chili powder
* ❖ ¼ cup olive oil
* ❖ 1 pasta bouillon cube (knorr)
* ❖ 3 cups water

Cooking Instructions:

* ❖ In a large saucepan, add olive oil, peppers, onion, meat and stir fry for 10 mins
* ❖ Add the Marinara sauce, chili powder and thyme and let it simmer for 5 mins
* ❖ Add the mixed vegetables and cook for 2 minutes
* ❖ Cover saucepan and set aside
* ❖ Add the spaghetti to water in a large saucepan
* ❖ Add the pasta bouillon cube and cook uncovered for 10 mins on high heat
* ❖ Drain spaghetti and toss
* ❖ Serve spaghetti in a pasta bowl with the sauce on top

Servings: 4
Per serving: 958 calories, 335 fat calories, 37.9g total fat, 10.3g saturated fat, 115mg cholesterol, 830mg sodium, 104.1g carbohydrate, 8.1g dietary fiber, 51.7g protein

Steamed Bean Cakes (Moin-Moin)

Moin-Moin is traditionally cooked in Nigeria by wrapping it in banana leaves and steaming it. Nowadays, it is cooked in aluminum muffin pans or meat loaf foil pans. There is no limit to what can be added to the recipe – beef liver, sliced boiled eggs, sardines etc.

Ingredients:

- ❖ 4 cups black eye beans
- ❖ 3/4 cup canola oil
- ❖ 1 red bell pepper
- ❖ 1 onion bulb
- ❖ 1 round hot chili pepper
- ❖ 2 large eggs well beaten
- ❖ 1 tablespoon salt
- ❖ 1 cup smoked or cooked prawns
- ❖ 1 cup corned beef
- ❖ 4 chicken bullion cubes

Cooking Instructions:

- ❖ Soak the beans in a bowl of warm water for 5 minutes
- ❖ Chop the beans in a blender for 2 minutes to split the beans and remove the skin
- ❖ Then rinse and sieve the beans in cold water until the skins have been removed
- ❖ Puree beans, pepper, water and onions in a blender, grind a little at a time unless it's a large blender
- ❖ Pour the mixture into a big mixing bowl
- ❖ Add 2 cups of water, crushed cubes, salt to taste, and mix with a wooden spoon
- ❖ Add the beaten egg, prawns and corn beef and mix well, then set aside
- ❖ Add 2-3 cups of water to a steamer and place on medium stove heat
- ❖ Grease about 15 meat loaf foil pans with oil
- ❖ Heat the oil in a sauce pan until very hot
- ❖ Add the hot oil to the bean mixture and stir into the beans

❖ Using a deep soupspoon, ladle the mixture in the loaf pans. Make sure that the loaf pan is only half full and cover each one

❖ Arrange the loaf pans in the steamer and cook for about 40-45 mins, adding water to the steamer if necessary.

❖ Turn moin-moin into a serving dish and garnish with sliced sweet peppers

❖ Serve as a main course or as a side with rice

Servings: 8
Per serving: 598 calories, 245 fat calories, 27.4g total fat, 4.1g saturated fat, 134mg cholesterol, 1273mg sodium, 53g carbohydrate, 9.5g dietary fiber, 35.3g protein

Cowpea Fritters (Akara)

These fritters (known as akara, bean balls, and kwasi) are breakfast favorites or snacks among the young and old in Nigeria. Akara is a very good source of protein and can be seen being sold as a fast food by vendors on the street, in marketplaces, and at bus stations. It is sometimes also fried in palm oil

Ingredients:

- 2 cups black eye beans
- 1 red bell pepper
- 1 onion bulb, chopped
- 1 round chili pepper, chopped (remove seeds)
- 1 large eggs well beaten
- 1 teaspoon salt
- 1 cup smoked or cooked prawns, tail off
- 1 chicken bullion cube
- 2 cups water

Cooking Instructions:

- Soak the beans in a bowl of warm water for 5 minutes
- Chop the beans in a blender for 2 minutes to split the beans and remove the skins
- Rinse and sieve the beans in cold water until all skins have been removed
- Puree beans and water in a blender, grind a little at a time unless it's a large blender
- Pour the mixture into a big mixing bowl
- Add 1 crumbled bouillon cube to bean mixture
- Add the onion, salt and chili pepper to the mixture and stir
- Add egg to mixture and stir well
- Fill the deep fat fryer to max mark with oil and preheat to 350F
- Spoon mixture in small ball sizes into hot oil, each ball ½ inch apart
- Cook balls until light brown on underside, flip and brown topside
- Serve hot with pap (ogi/akamu), or custard for breakfast

Servings: 8
Per serving: 466 calories, 117 fat calories, 13g total fat, 2.9g saturated fat, 105mg cholesterol, 671mg sodium, 52.8g carbohydrate, 9.6g dietary fiber, 34.4g protein

Yam Fritters (Ojojo)

Ingredients:

- ❖ 1 kg. freshwater yam
- ❖ 1 tablespoon chili pepper
- ❖ 1 onion bulb, chopped
- ❖ 1 teaspoon salt
- ❖ 1 cup smoked or cooked prawns, tail off
- ❖ 1 chicken bouillon cube

Cooking Instructions:

- ❖ Peel, wash and grate yam
- ❖ Add salt, pepper and chopped onion, mix well
- ❖ Add shrimps and crushed bouillon cube, mixing very well
- ❖ Fill the deep fat fryer to min mark with oil and preheat to 350F
- ❖ Ladle mixture in small ball sizes into hot oil, each ball ½ inch apart
- ❖ Cook balls until light brown on underside, flip and brown topside
- ❖ Serve hot with pap (ogi/akamu), or custard

Servings: 8
Per serving: 247 calories, 67 fat calories, 7.7g total fat, 0.6g saturated fat, 57mg cholesterol, 384mg sodium, 36.6g carbohydrate, 5.6g dietary fiber, 8.3g protein

Traditional Nigerian Bean Casserole (Ewa Riro)

Ingredients:

- ❖ 4 cups Nigerian brown hybrid beans
- ❖ 2 ripe Plantains, peeled and cubed
- ❖ 8 oz frozen sweet corn (optional)
- ❖ 8 cups of water
- ❖ 1½ teaspoon salt
- ❖ 2 beef bouillon cubes
- ❖ 3 tablespoon palm oil
- ❖ 1 tablespoon chili powder
- ❖ 2 tablespoon olive oil
- ❖ 1 teaspoon season all

Cooking Instructions:

- ❖ Add 4 cups of water and beans in a large pressure cooker
- ❖ Cover and cook for 15-20 minutes
- ❖ Rinse the beans in warm water to get rid of the brown water
- ❖ Add 2 cups of water to it, cover and cook on medium high for 10 minutes
- ❖ Add the plantain, salt, bullion cubes and season all
- ❖ Cook the beans for another 15-20 minutes until very soft adding water if needed
- ❖ Add the chili powder, palm oil and olive oil and stir well
- ❖ Cover and let it cook for another 5 minutes stirring occasionally
- ❖ Serve hot with a side of fried plantain

Servings: 8
Per serving: 447 calories, 89 fat calories, 10.1g total fat, 3.4g saturated fat, 0mg cholesterol, 478mg sodium, 68.5g carbohydrate, 10.9g dietary fiber, 21.1g protein

Jerk Chicken

Jamaican Jerk Seasoning is a spicy, tangy seasoning. Its unique flavor is fast becoming popular with American consumers in all walks of life. There are many variations in the US market but the authentic is the paste that can be rubbed on chicken

Ingredients:

- 12 pieces chicken drum sticks/wings
- 4 tablespoon Jerk seasoning powder
- 1 teaspoon season all or allspice
- 1 cup diced onion
- 1 cup diced scallions
- 1 teaspoon thyme
- 1 teaspoon parsley
- 2 hot bonnet pepper (seeded and chopped)
- 1 teaspoon salt
- 1 teaspoon cracked black pepper
- 2 tablespoon Worcestershire sauce
- 1 cup olive oil
- 2 tablespoon warm water

Cooking Instructions:

- Puree all ingredients except chicken in a blender and chill in the refrigerator overnight
- Rinse the chicken parts in water and pat dry
- Put chicken in a ziploc bag and pour chilled spices on it, swirl to coat chicken
- Refrigerate overnight to allow the chicken to absorb the full flavor
- Preheat the oven to 375F
- Arrange in a greased baking pan (I use olive oil spray). Cover with foil and make 2 slits in the foil
- Bake for 30 mins, then remove the foil and drain the juices into a dip bowl
- Set the oven to broil and broil chicken for 10-15 minutes or until medium brown
- Serve chicken as an appetizer or as a side with steamed rice

Servings: 6
Per serving: 449 calories, 180 fat calories, 20.2g total fat, 4.1g saturated fat, 229mg cholesterol, 886mg sodium, 4g carbohydrate, 2.3g dietary fiber, 63.2g protein

Tangy Chicken

The lemon juice and season-all gives this chicken its tangy taste. This delicacy is best served with steamed rice and tangy coleslaw

Ingredients:

- ❖ 2½ lb. broiler chicken
- ❖ 1 red bell pepper, sliced
- ❖ 1 green bell pepper, sliced
- ❖ 1 yellow bell pepper, sliced
- ❖ 1 medium onion, sliced
- ❖ 1 tablespoon malt vinegar
- ❖ 3 tablespoon olive oil
- ❖ 2 chicken bouillon cubes
- ❖ 1 large lemon
- ❖ 1 medium tomato, sliced
- ❖ ¼ teaspoon chili powder
- ❖ ½ teaspoon salt
- ❖ ½ teaspoon season all
- ❖ splash of Worcestershire sauce
- ❖ ½ cup warm water

Cooking Instructions:

- ❖ Wash and cut chicken into parts
- ❖ Cut lemon into two halves and squeeze the juice on chicken
- ❖ Add Worcestershire sauce, salt, season all and vinegar to chicken
- ❖ Marinade chicken for 1 hour in the refrigerator
- ❖ Add olive oil in a large saucepan on medium high
- ❖ Add chicken to olive oil and stir fry on high for 10 minutes
- ❖ Add peppers, onion, tomato, chili powder to chicken on high for 5 minutes, stirring occasionally
- ❖ Reduce heat to medium low and add water
- ❖ Cover saucepan and cook chicken for 10-15 minutes
- ❖ Serve hot on steamed rice with a side of tangy coleslaw

Servings: 6
Per serving: 311 calories, 115 fat calories, 12.8g total fat, 2.2g saturated fat, 132mg cholesterol, 352mg sodium, 7.6g carbohydrate, 1.7g dietary fiber, 41.5g protein

Grilled Salmon Steak

Ingredients:

- ❖ Two 10 oz salmon steaks
- ❖ ½ cup olive oil
- ❖ 1 tablespoon lemon juice
- ❖ 2 teaspoon fresh or dried chopped parsley
- ❖ ½ teaspoon pepper (or to taste)
- ❖ ¼ cup Chinese light soy sauce
- ❖ Ground clove

Cooking Instructions:

- ❖ Combine olive oil, soy sauce, parsley, lemon juice, pepper and clove
- ❖ Brush over the salmon steaks
- ❖ Arrange steaks in a lightly greased small baking dish
- ❖ Broil steaks on both sides for 10-15 minutes until lightly browned and tender
- ❖ It is cooked when it loses its translucency and becomes flaky
- ❖ Serve hot on caesar salad or with mashed potatoes

Servings: 8
Per serving: 206 calories, 144 fat calories, 15.9g total fat, 2.2g saturated fat, 37mg cholesterol, 313mg sodium, 0.9g carbohydrate, 0.1g dietary fiber, 14.5g protein

Slow Cooking Meat Loaf

Ingredients:

- ❖ ½ cup whole milk
- ❖ 2 slices white bread
- ❖ 1½ lb. ground beef
- ❖ 2 eggs
- ❖ 1 small onion, peeled
- ❖ 1½ teaspoon salt
- ❖ 1½ teaspoon pepper
- ❖ 1 teaspoon dry mustard
- ❖ 1 can (12 oz.) whole tomatoes, drained

Cooking Instructions:

- ❖ Add milk and bread in a large mixing bowl, set aside until bread has absorbed all the milk
- ❖ With two forks, break the bread into crumbs
- ❖ Beat the ground beef into the crumbs until well mixed
- ❖ Make a hollow in the center of the meat and break the eggs into it
- ❖ Slightly beat the eggs and add onions to the eggs
- ❖ Add salt, pepper and mustard to taste
- ❖ Beat the eggs into the beef and shape into a round mould
- ❖ Place in the slow cooker and add the tomatoes
- ❖ Cover and cook on Low for 5-7 hours
- ❖ Remove the lid and increase heat to high to steam out some of the sauce
- ❖ Slice and serve hot with mashed potatoes

Servings: 6
Per serving: 339 calories, 200 fat calories, 22g total fat, 8.5g saturated fat, 152mg cholesterol, 703mg sodium, 9.2g carbohydrate, 1.1g dietary fiber, 25.6g protein

Slow Cooking Barbecue Steak

Ingredients:

- ❖ 1½ lb. boneless chuck steak or ribs
- ❖ 1 clove garlic, peeled and minced
- ❖ ¼ cup wine vinegar
- ❖ 1 tablespoon brown sugar
- ❖ 1 teaspoon paprika
- ❖ 2 tablespoons Worcestershire sauce
- ❖ ½ cup catsup
- ❖ 1 teaspoon salt
- ❖ 1 teaspoon dry or prepared mustard
- ❖ ¼ teaspoon black pepper

Cooking Instructions:

- ❖ Cut the beef on a diagonal, across the grain into slices 1 inch wide
- ❖ Place the beef in a slow cooker
- ❖ In a small bowl, combine the remaining ingredients and pour over meat
- ❖ Cover and cook on low for 3-5 hours
- ❖ Serve hot with mashed potatoes or some fries

Servings: 4
Per serving: 332 calories, 132 fat calories, 14.4g total fat, 4.8g saturated fat, 102mg cholesterol, 372mg sodium, 14g carbohydrate, 1g dietary fiber, 35.8g protein

Slow Cooking Tasty Leg-of-Lamb

Ingredients:

- ❖ 1 half leg of lamb, butterflied
- ❖ ¼ cup soy sauce
- ❖ ¾ cup pinot noir (Burgundy)
- ❖ ¼ cup orange juice
- ❖ 2 tablespoons lemon juice
- ❖ 2 tablespoons honey
- ❖ 1 teaspoon dry mustard
- ❖ 1 cup tomato puree
- ❖ 3 cloves garlic
- ❖ ¼ teaspoon ground black pepper

Cooking Instructions:

- ❖ Place the lamb in a large glass bowl
- ❖ Mix all the other ingredients together in a mixing bowl
- ❖ Pour the marinade over the lamb
- ❖ Cover and marinate in the refrigerator for 12 hours, turning occasionally
- ❖ Place the lamb in a slow cooker and cook for 7-8 hours on low
- ❖ Slice thin and serve with garlic mashed potatoes and some vegetables

Servings: 8
Per serving: 409 calories, 133 fat calories, 14.7g total fat, 5.1g saturated fat, 190mg cholesterol, 458mg sodium, 9.5g carbohydrate, 0.9g dietary fiber, 59.6g protein

Tender and Spicy Baby Back Ribs

Why wait to get to a restaurant to enjoy baby back ribs? These ribs are so juicy and tender; they fall off the bones.

Ingredients:

- ❖ 2lb. pork baby back ribs
- ❖ 1 (18 ounce) bottle barbecue sauce
- ❖ ¼ teaspoon ground black pepper
- ❖ ¼ teaspoon ground white pepper
- ❖ 1 tablespoon sweet cayenne
- ❖ 1 teaspoon crushed garlic
- ❖ ½ teaspoon season-all

Cooking Instructions:

- ❖ Mix cayenne, garlic, season-all, white and black pepper in a bowl
- ❖ Coat ribs with sweet cayenne and garlic mixture
- ❖ Brush the ribs liberally with barbecue sauce
- ❖ Tear off 4 pieces of aluminum foil big enough to enclose each portion of ribs
- ❖ Spray each piece of foil with canola cooking spray
- ❖ Place each rib portion in a piece of foil and wrap tightly
- ❖ Preheat oven to 300F and bake ribs for 2-2½ hours
- ❖ Remove from foil, add more sauce, if desired and broil for 5-10 minutes
- ❖ Serve with garlic mashed potatoes or breadfruit fries and some vegetables

Servings: 4
Per serving: 734 calories, 502 fat calories, 56g total fat, 20g saturated fat, 184mg cholesterol, 1197mg sodium, 16g carbohydrate, 2g dietary fiber, 39g protein

Honey and Garlic Ribs

Ingredients:

- ❖ 4 lb. pork spareribs
- ❖ ½ cup orange blossom honey
- ❖ ¼ cup soy sauce (reduced sodium)
- ❖ 1/4 cup distilled white vinegar
- ❖ 2 cloves garlic, minced
- ❖ 2 tablespoons brown sugar
- ❖ 1 teaspoon garlic salt
- ❖ 1 teaspoon baking soda

Cooking Instructions:

- ❖ Slice the ribs into individual pieces
- ❖ Combine honey, soy sauce, vinegar, garlic and brown sugar in a large bowl
- ❖ Stir until honey and sugar are completely dissolved
- ❖ Stir in the baking soda and mixture should begin to foam
- ❖ Transfer ribs to the bowl, and coat with mixture
- ❖ Cover a cookie sheet with foil, and arrange the ribs meat side up on the sheet
- ❖ Pour excess sauce over ribs and sprinkle with the garlic salt
- ❖ Preheat oven to 375F and bake ribs for 1 hour turning every 20 minutes
- ❖ Serve with garlic mashed potatoes or breadfruit fries and some vegetables. The sauce is also delicious on steamed rice

Servings: 4
Per serving: 368 calories, 211 fat calories, 23g total fat, 9g saturated fat, 77mg cholesterol, 596mg sodium, 22g carbohydrate, 0g dietary fiber, 18g protein

Creamy Garlic Mashed Potato

Ingredients:

- ❖ 3 lbs. Russet potatoes, peeled, washed and cut into 2 inch chunks
- ❖ 6 quarts filtered water
- ❖ ½ lb. unsalted butter
- ❖ 3 teaspoons kosher salt
- ❖ 1 tablespoon garlic, crushed
- ❖ Salt to taste
- ❖ 1½ cup heavy cream
- ❖ ½ cup half & half
- ❖ 3 tablespoon milk (to lighten the mashed potato)
- ❖ 1 teaspoon white pepper, ground
- ❖ 1 teaspoon ground nutmeg

Cooking Instructions:

- ❖ Add water above potato level in a large pot and add salt
- ❖ Bring to a boil and reduce the heat to medium low
- ❖ Cook for 30-40 minutes or until tender
- ❖ Drain potatoes dry in a colander and return to pot
- ❖ Melt ½ cup of butter with the garlic over low heat
- ❖ Add the butter mixture, cream and seasonings to potatoes and mash
- ❖ Add butter on top to melt and warm mashed potatoes for 2 minutes on low
- ❖ Serve hot with steamed vegetables and grilled salmon

Servings: 8
Per serving: 462 calories, 302 fat calories, 33.4g total fat, 20.8g saturated fat, 99mg cholesterol, 639mg sodium, 35.7g carbohydrate, 3.2g dietary fiber, 4.2g protein

Shepherd's Pie

Ingredients:

- 1½ lb. ground lamb or beef
- 1 medium yellow onion, sliced thinly
- 1½ cups mashed potatoes
- ½ cup carrots, cooked and diced
- 1 cup meat broth or onion gravy
- 2 tablespoons melted butter
- salt and pepper to taste

Cooking Instructions:

- Brown onions thoroughly in large skillet
- Add ground lamb or beef, cook until browned, stirring frequently
- Add stock or gravy, and season to taste
- Layer carrots and meat in 5-quart casserole dish
- Top with mashed potatoes
- Drizzle melted butter on top, and criss-cross with a fork
- Preheat oven to 350°F and bake for 40-45 minutes or until potato is browned

Servings: 4
Per serving: 540 calories, 323 fat calories, 35.7g total fat, 15.5g saturated fat, 138mg cholesterol, 703mg sodium, 19g carbohydrate, 3.2g dietary fiber, 35.3g protein

Fisherman's Pie

Ingredients:

- 10 oz white fish (haddock, cod)
- 6 oz prawns
- 1½ lb. potatoes
- ½ oz butter or margarine
- 2 oz hot milk
- Salt and pepper
- 1 egg, beaten

Sauce:

- 1 oz butter or margarine
- 1 oz flour
- 1 cup milk
- 1 tablespoon chopped parsley
- Salt and pepper

Cooking Instructions:

- Skin and bone fish, cut into fairly large chunks
- Wash fish and prawns, and dry on kitchen paper towel
- Peel potatoes and cook in boiling salted water until tender
- Drain potatoes in a colander, mash and beat in butter, hot milk and seasoning
- Combine white sauce ingredients in a bowl, add parsley and season to taste
- Arrange fish and prawns in a casserole dish and top with the white sauce
- Top with even layer of potato
- Preheat oven to 375F and bake for 30 minutes
- Brush top of potato with the beaten egg
- Bake for an additional 20-30 minutes
- Serve hot

Servings: 4
Per serving: 297 calories, 57 fat calories, 6g total fat, 2.5g saturated fat, 166mg cholesterol, 292mg sodium, 32g carbohydrate, 3.1g dietary fiber, 28g protein

Curry Goat

Goat meat is lean, low in fat and cholesterol, and if prepared correctly should be sweet and tender due to its higher moisture content. Compared to Beef, Goat is high in protein, but low in calories, fat and cholesterol.

Ingredients:

- ❖ 3 lb. goat meat
- ❖ 2 medium onions diced
- ❖ 4 cloves garlic
- ❖ 1 teaspoon black pepper
- ❖ ½ lb. diced Irish potato
- ❖ Fresh thyme
- ❖ 3 tablespoon authentic Jamaican curry powder
- ❖ 1 tablespoon butter
- ❖ 1 teaspoon ground pimento
- ❖ 4 scallions diced
- ❖ 1 scotch bonnet pepper finely cut
- ❖ ¼ teaspoon salt
- ❖ 3 tablespoon olive oil
- ❖ 2 cups hot water

Cooking Instructions:

- ❖ Cut goat meat into bite size cubes, rinse and pat dry
- ❖ Season meat with salt, black pepper, crushed garlic, scallion and diced onions
- ❖ Add 2 tablespoon curry powder and mix well
- ❖ Leave to marinade overnight
- ❖ Remove the seasonings (onions, scallions, crushed garlic) and brown meat in small amount of olive oil
- ❖ Add 2 cups of hot water, scallions and crushed garlic
- ❖ Cook over medium heat for 35 – 40 minutes until fork tender
- ❖ Add 1 tablespoon of curry powder, the butter and diced potatoes
- ❖ Add the onions 10 – 15 minutes before removing from the stove
- ❖ Serve hot on a bed of steamed rice and vegetables

Servings: 8
Per serving: 300 calories, 111 fat calories, 12.3g total fat, 3g saturated fat, 100mg cholesterol, 221mg sodium, 10.8g carbohydrate, 1.9g dietary fiber, 36.5g protein

Curry Pork

Ingredients:

- ½ lb. Pork
- 2 medium onions diced
- 4 cloves garlic
- 2-inch piece ginger
- 2 medium tomatoes
- 2 tablespoons vinegar
- 2 teaspoons salt
- ½ teaspoon garam marsala
- 1 tablespoon hot vindaloo paste
- 2 medium potatoes, peeled and cubed
- 2 cups water

Cooking Instructions:

- Cut pork into 1 inch cubes, rinse and pat dry
- Mix marsala, onions, ginger, salt and tomatoes in a small bowl
- Pour mixture into a large saucepan, add vinegar, water and vindaloo paste
- Cook for 2 minutes, stirring and add the pork
- Cover and for 1½ hours on low heat until the pieces are tender
- Add potatoes, and cook for 30 minutes
- Serve hot on a bed of steamed rice and vegetables

Servings: 6
Per serving: 95 calories, 21 fat calories, 2.3g total fat, 0.7g saturated fat, 23mg cholesterol, 811mg sodium, 9.2g carbohydrate, 1.6g dietary fiber, 9.3g protein

Curry Prawn

Ingredients:

- ❖ 1 lb. jumbo prawns
- ❖ 2 medium onions diced
- ❖ ¼ teaspoon garlic powder
- ❖ ½ teaspoon ginger powder
- ❖ 1 bunch fresh coriander
- ❖ ¼ inch cinnamon stick
- ❖ 1 teaspoon salt
- ❖ ¼ teaspoon chili powder
- ❖ ¼ teaspoon turmeric powder
- ❖ ½ teaspoon dhania powder
- ❖ 1 tablespoon canola oil

Cooking Instructions:

- ❖ Clean the prawns and squeeze out excess water
- ❖ Add chili, dhania, garlic, ginger, turmeric, black pepper, and salt in a small bowl
- ❖ Add 1 teaspoon of oil to the prawns and boil on low heat
- ❖ When water evaporates and the prawns are dry remove from the stove
- ❖ Heat the oil and put in the cinnamon
- ❖ Add prawns and fry for 2 minutes
- ❖ Add onions and continue to fry until they turn brown
- ❖ Sprinkle on coriander leaves
- ❖ Serve hot on a bed of steamed rice and vegetables

Servings: 6
Per serving: 111 calories, 33 fat calories, 3.7g total fat, 0.4g saturated fat, 114mg cholesterol, 507mg sodium, 3.7g carbohydrate, 1.1g dietary fiber, 15.9g protein

Edikan-ikong

Ingredients:

- ❖ 6 oz Pumpkin leaves, chopped
- ❖ 4 oz Waterleaf, chopped
- ❖ 1 lb. lean beef or goat
- ❖ ½ lb. dried fish
- ❖ ½ lb. stockfish (optional)
- ❖ ½ lb. shrimp (optional)
- ❖ ½ lb. snails (optional)
- ❖ 2 cups periwinkle (shelled)
- ❖ ½ lb. tripe
- ❖ ½ lb. ox tail
- ❖ ½ lb. cow kidney
- ❖ 4 tablespoons ground crayfish
- ❖ 2 bouillon cubes
- ❖ ½ cup palm oil
- ❖ 1 teaspoon salt
- ❖ 1 tablespoon chili pepper
- ❖ ½ teaspoon season-all
- ❖ 1 cup water

Cooking Instructions:

- ❖ Cut and add oxtail, tripe, kidney, and lean meat in a large saucepan
- ❖ Add the seasonings, bouillon cubes and cook for 20-25 minutes on medium high
- ❖ Strain off broth and set aside
- ❖ Add half of palm oil in a large saucepan and heat on medium for 2 minutes
- ❖ Add pumpkin and water leaves, cover and steam for 5 minutes
- ❖ Reduce heat to medium low and stir
- ❖ Add all the meat, fish, shrimps, periwinkle and crayfish stirring
- ❖ Let it simmer for 10 minutes
- ❖ Add the broth, pepper, remaining palmoil, bouillon cubes and onions
- ❖ Stir through and let it simmer for 3 minutes
- ❖ Serve hot with fufu, eba or pounded yam

Servings: 8
Per serving: 279 calories, 87 fat calories, 10g total fat, 4.1g saturated fat, 260mg cholesterol, 352mg sodium, 2.9g carbohydrate, 1.3g dietary fiber, 45g protein

Ogbono

Ogbono or Apon is the whole or crushed kernels of the bush mango, or wild mango tree (Irvingia gabonensis or Irvingia wombolu), which is native to the tropical Atlantic coast region of Africa.

Ingredients:

- ½ cup canola oil
- 2 medium onions, diced
- 1lb. beef (goat/lamb as a variation), bite-sized pieces
- 1 teaspoon chili powder
- 1 hot chili pepper, diced
- ½ cup palm oil (optional)
- 2 medium tomatoes, diced
- 2 oz crayfish, ground
- 2 oz crab meat
- 2 oz smoked prawns
- 4 oz smoked tilapia or cod
- ½ cup Ogbono, ground
- 2 beef bouillon cubes
- 8 oz bitter leaves, chopped
- salt (to taste)
- 3 cups water
- 2 tablespoons melon seeds, ground

Cooking Instructions:

- Sprinkle chili powder on the meat, stir and marinade for 30 minutes
- Add water in a large saucepan and bring to a boil
- Add all meat and cook for 25-30 minutes on medium high
- Reduce heat to medium, cover and simmer for 10-15 minutes
- Add ½ cup of oil in a skillet and stir fry tomatoes, chili pepper and onion
- Add the stir fry to the meat and cover
- Let it simmer for 5-10 minutes on medium low
- Heat ½ cup oil in a skillet and stir in the ogbono and melon to form a paste
- Add the ogbono paste to meat and stir briskly to avoid lumps
- Add fish, bouillon cubes, prawns, crayfish, and crabmeat
- Sprinkle with bitter leaf and let simmer for 5-10 minutes
- Serve with Fufu, Pounded yam, or Amala

Servings: 6
Per serving: 235 calories, 59 fat calories, 6.5g total fat, 1.1g saturated fat, 65mg cholesterol, 712mg sodium, 15.1g carbohydrate, 2.4g dietary fiber, 29.1g protein

Yam Stew (Ikokore)

Cocoyam is used in essentially the same way as yam. It can be eaten boiled, fried or pounded into fufu, although it is not considered as prestigious as yam. It can also be made into porridge or pottage, as well as chips and flour. Cocoyam flour has the added advantage that it is highly digestible and so is used for invalids and as an ingredient in baby foods.

Ingredients:

- 1 medium water yam
- 2 teaspoons ground chili pepper
- 2 teaspoons locust beans
- 1 teaspoon onion salt
- 1 lb. lean meat, diced
- 2 cups beef broth
- 1 cup smoked shrimp
- 5 tablespoons ground crayfish
- 1/3 cup palm oil
- 2 cups smoked dry fish
- 2 chicken bullion cubes
- ¼ teaspoon season-all
- 1 cup water

Cooking Instructions:

- Peel, wash and grate yam in a large mixing bowl
- Soak fish in hot water, remove the bones, flake fish and set aside
- Add meat, seasonings and a cup of water in a large saucepan
- Cover and cook for 25 minutes on medium low
- Add fish and shrimps to meat and cook for 5 minutes
- Remove meat and shrimp from broth, set aside
- Add pepper, crayfish and water to broth and cook for 2 minutes
- Make grated yam into small balls and add to stew
- Add the meat and fish
- Cover and simmer for 20-30 minutes until cooked through
- Add palm oil and let it cook for 5 minutes, stirring
- Serve hot

Servings: 8
Per serving: 349 calories, 114 fat calories, 12.9g total fat, 5.7g saturated fat, 134mg cholesterol, 662mg sodium, 24.1g carbohydrate, 3.7g dietary fiber, 34.7g protein

Deserts

Crème Brûlée Classic

Ingredients:

- ❖ 8 egg yolks
- ❖ 1/3 cup granulated white sugar
- ❖ 2 cups heavy cream
- ❖ 1 teaspoon pure vanilla extract
- ❖ 1/4 cup granulated white sugar (for the caramelized tops)

Baking Instructions:

- ❖ Preheat oven to 300°F
- ❖ In a large bowl, whisk together egg yolks and sugar until the sugar has dissolved and the mixture is thick and pale yellow
- ❖ Add cream and vanilla, and continue to whisk until well blended.
- ❖ Strain into a large bowl, skimming off any foam or bubbles.
- ❖ Divide mixture among 6 ramekins or custard cups
- ❖ Place in a water bath and bake until set around the edges, but still loose in the center, about 45 to 50 minutes
- ❖ Remove from oven and leave in the water bath until cooled
- ❖ Remove cups from water bath and chill for at least 2 hours, or up to 2 days
- ❖ Sprinkle about 2 teaspoons of sugar on top when ready to serve. For best results, use a small, hand-held torch to melt sugar or place under the broiler until sugar melts
- ❖ Re-chill custards for a few minutes before serving.

Servings: 6
Per serving: 246 calories, 163 fat calories, 18.2g total fat, 9.5g saturated fat, 283mg cholesterol, 25mg sodium, 16.7g carbohydrate, 0g dietary fiber, 4g protein

Coffee – Brandy Crème Brûlée

Ingredients:

- 2 cups whipping cream
- ¼ cup sugar
- 1 ½ teaspoon instant coffee crystals
- 4 large egg yolks
- 1 tablespoon brandy
- 1 teaspoon vanilla extract
- 3 tablespoon (packed) golden brown sugar

Baking Instructions:

- Preheat oven to 350°F
- Arrange six ¾ -cup ramekins or custard cups in 13x9x2-inch metal baking pan
- Combine cream and ¼ cup sugar in heavy medium saucepan, bring almost to simmer, and stir until sugar dissolves
- Remove from heat, add coffee and whisk to dissolve
- Whisk egg yolks in medium bowl
- Gradually whisk in warm cream mixture, then brandy and vanilla
- Strain custard into 4-cup measuring cup; divide equally in the ramekins
- Pour enough hot water into pan to come halfway up sides of ramekins
- Bake custards until center moves only slightly when pan is gently shaken, about 35 minutes
- Remove custards from pan, chill until cold, at least 3 hours, and then cover and keep chilled overnight
- Preheat broiler. Arrange custards on baking sheet
- Sprinkle ½ tablespoon brown sugar on each, forming an even layer.
- Broil 6 inches from heat source until sugar melts, bubbles and caramelizes, watching carefully and rotating sheet for even browning, about 4 minutes
- Refrigerate custards until sugar topping hardens, at least 1 hour and up to 4 hours before serving.

Servings: 6
Per serving: 255 calories, 150 fat calories, 16.2g total fat, 8.2g saturated fat, 260mg cholesterol, 25mg sodium, 16.7g carbohydrate, 0g dietary fiber, 4g protein

Tiramisu' Classic

Tiramisu', also known as "Tuscan Trifle," was initially created in Siena, in the northwestern Italian province of Tuscany. It was later introduced to Treviso, near Venice, about 20 years ago a place best known for its canals, frescoes and Tiramisu. Custard was used in the original recipe and only recently has Mascarpone cheese been substituted Widely popular, there are as many versions of Tiramisu' today as there are cooks who make it!

Ingredients:

* ❖ 4 tablespoon rum, or to taste (optional)
* ❖ 1/3 cup coffee flavored liqueur
* ❖ 2 tablespoon brandy (optional)
* ❖ 2 (12 oz) packages ladyfingers (savoiardi)
* ❖ 1¼ cups mascarpone
* ❖ 6 eggs, yolks and whites separated
* ❖ 1¼ cups confectioners' sugar
* ❖ 1 oz semi sweet chocolate
* ❖ 1 teaspoon unsweetened cocoa powder
* ❖ 1¾ cups heavy whipping cream

Baking Instructions:

* ❖ Arrange the lady fingers in a shallow dish
* ❖ Mix 2 tablespoons of the rum with the coffee liqueur and brandy
* ❖ Sprinkle mixture on the ladyfingers, they should be very moist but not soggy
* ❖ Combine egg yolks and sugar in a glass bowl, over boiling water
* ❖ Cook for 10 minutes, stirring. Turn off heat and whip until thick and lemon colored.
* ❖ Add mascarpone and remaining rum to whipped yolks, beat until combined
* ❖ In a separate bowl, whip cream to stiff peaks and fold into yolk mixture
* ❖ Spoon half of the cream filling over lady fingers
* ❖ Repeat ladyfingers, liqueur splash and filling layers
* ❖ Refrigerate several hours or overnight
* ❖ Sprinkle with powdered cocoa and garnish with chocolate curls just before serving

Servings: 10
Per serving: 689 calories, 346 fat calories, 38g total fat, 20g saturated fat, 466mg cholesterol, 136mg sodium, 72g carbohydrate, 1g dietary fiber, 12g protein

Signature Rum Carrot Cake

Ingredients:

- 2 cups sifted flour
- 3 teaspoon cinnamon
- 2 teaspoon baking powder
- 1½ teaspoon baking soda
- 1 teaspoon salt
- 4 large eggs
- 1 ½ cups canola oil
- 2 cups light brown sugar
- 2 ¾ cups coarsely grated carrots
- 1 cup shredded sweetened coconut
- ¾ cup chopped pecans
- 8 oz can crushed pineapple drained
- 1 cup Jamaican brown rum
- 1 cup mixed fruit or raisins

For Cream Cheese Frosting

- ½ cup butter/margarine
- 1 ½ teaspoon bourbon vanilla
- 1 lb. confectioner's sugar
- 8 oz package cream cheese

Baking Instructions:

- Sift flour in a mixing bowl, add baking powder, soda, cinnamon and salt
- In another bowl, mix oil, sugar and eggs together adding the flour mixture to it little at a time. Mix well after each addition
- Add carrots, coconut, pineapple, nuts, raisins, rum and mix very well
- Turn into a 9 x 12 greased and lightly floured deep cake pan
- Preheat oven at 350F and bake for 35 – 40 minutes
- Let the cake cool for 15 minutes before turning. Let it cool completely before adding cheese frosting
- Cream butter and cheese together with vanilla
- Add confectioner's sugar and mix very well
- Spread on cake and refrigerate before serving

Servings: 12
Per serving: 892 calories, 404 fat calories, 44.9g total fat, 6.8g saturated fat, 71mg cholesterol, 524mg sodium, 113.4g carbohydrate, 3.5g dietary fiber, 8.6g protein

Moist Signature Banana Pound Cake

Ingredients:

- ❖ 1 cup white sugar
- ❖ 1 lb. brown sugar
- ❖ 1 lb. butter
- ❖ 5 eggs
- ❖ ½ teaspoon salt
- ❖ 1 teaspoon vanilla
- ❖ 1 teaspoon cinnamon
- ❖ 2 tablespoon Jamaican rum (*optional*)
- ❖ 1 cup pecans
- ❖ 1 cup raisins /craisins
- ❖ ½ cup granola
- ❖ 3 cup flour
- ❖ 1 cup 2% reduced fat milk
- ❖ ½ teaspoon baking powder
- ❖ 2 large over ripe banana mashed

Baking Instructions:

- ❖ Cream the sugar and butter until light and very fluffy
- ❖ Add one egg at a time to the mixture and mix very well after each addition
- ❖ Next add the mashed bananas and mix well
- ❖ In a bowl, combine the flour, baking powder, cinnamon and salt. In another bowl, combine milk and vanilla
- ❖ Add the flour mixture and milk alternately to the cream mixture mixing well after each addition. If mixture curdles, add some flour
- ❖ Stir in the pecans and raisins
- ❖ Preheat oven to 350F
- ❖ Pour cake mixture into a deep 12" well greased tube cake pan
- ❖ Bake for 60-90 minutes or until a skewer inserted into the center comes out clean. Oven temperatures may vary depending on the type of oven
- ❖ Cool on a rack and serve cold or warm with vanilla ice cream

Servings: 12
Per serving: 813 calories, 378 fat calories, 42g total fat, 21.3g saturated fat, 173mg cholesterol, 491mg sodium, 100g carbohydrate, 2.9g dietary fiber, 8.8g protein

Sweet Honey Bun Cake

Ingredients:

- ❖ 1 (18.5 oz) package yellow cake mix
- ❖ ¾ cup vegetable oil
- ❖ 4 eggs
- ❖ 1 (8 oz) container sour cream
- ❖ 1 cup brown sugar
- ❖ 1 tablespoon ground cinnamon
- ❖ 2 cups confectioners' sugar
- ❖ ¼ cup milk
- ❖ 1 tablespoon vanilla extract

Baking Instructions:

- ❖ Combine cake mix, oil, eggs and sour cream in a large mixing bowl
- ❖ Stir manually (approximately 50 strokes) until most large lumps are gone
- ❖ Pour half of the batter into an ungreased 9x13 inch glass baking dish
- ❖ Combine the brown sugar and cinnamon, and sprinkle over the batter in the cake pan.
- ❖ Spoon the remaining batter into the cake pan to cover brown sugar and cinnamon
- ❖ Twirl the cake with a icing knife to give a honey bun shape
- ❖ Preheat oven to 325F
- ❖ Bake for 40 minutes, or until a skewer inserted into the center comes out clean
- ❖ In a small bowl, whisk together the confectioner's sugar, milk and vanilla until smooth to make a frost
- ❖ Frost cake while it is still fairly hot
- ❖ Serve warm

Servings: 24
Per serving: 252 calories, 110 fat calories, 12g total fat, .3g saturated fat, 40mg cholesterol, 163mg sodium, 34g carbohydrate, 0g dietary fiber, 2g protein

Heavenly Pound Cake

Ingredients:

- ½ cup shortening
- 1 cup butter
- 2½ cups white sugar
- 5 eggs
- 2 teaspoons almond extract
- 1 cup milk
- ½ teaspoon baking powder
- 3 cups wholemeal flour
- 1 teaspoon ground cinnamon

Baking Instructions:

- Cream shortening, butter and sugar until light and fluffy using electric mixer
- Add eggs, one at a time, beating well after each addition
- Beat in almond extract
- Combine baking powder, cinnamon and flour in a mixing bowl
- Stir flour into creamed mixture alternating with the milk
- Lightly grease and flour a 10-inch cake pan
- Pour batter into cake pan
- Preheat oven to 300F
- Bake in the preheated oven for 75 minutes or until a skewer inserted into the center comes out clean
- Allow cake to cool in pan for 10 minutes, then turn out onto a wire rack
- Serve plain or with strawberries and cream

Servings: 12
Per serving: 547 calories, 240 fat calories, 27g total fat, 13g saturated fat, 131mg cholesterol, 214mg sodium, 71g carbohydrate, 1g dietary fiber, 6g protein

Lemony Pound Cake

Ingredients:

- ❖ 3 cups all-purpose flour
- ❖ ¾ teaspoon baking powder
- ❖ ¼ teaspoon salt
- ❖ 1 cup unsalted butter, softened
- ❖ ½ cup shortening
- ❖ 2 2/3 cups white sugar
- ❖ 5 eggs
- ❖ 1 cup milk
- ❖ 1 teaspoon vanilla extract
- ❖ 1 teaspoon lemon extract (add more to taste)

Baking Instructions:

- ❖ Combine the sifted flour, baking powder and salt in a mixing bowl and set aside
- ❖ Beat butter, shortening, and sugar together on low speed for 10 minutes
- ❖ Add eggs, one at a time, beating well after each addition
- ❖ Stir flour into creamed mixture alternating with the milk
- ❖ Beat in almond and vanilla extracts
- ❖ Lightly grease a 10-inch tube cake pan and line bottom with parchment paper
- ❖ Pour batter into cake pan
- ❖ Bake at 350F for 80 minutes or until a skewer inserted into the center comes out clean
- ❖ Allow cake to cool in the pan for 30 minutes
- ❖ Serve plain or with vanilla ice cream

Servings: 14
Per serving: 462 calories, 206 fat calories, 23g total fat, 11g saturated fat, 113mg cholesterol, 102mg sodium, 60g carbohydrate, 1g dietary fiber, 6g protein

Orange Pound Cake

Ingredients:

- ❖ 1 (18.5 oz) package yellow cake mix
- ❖ 1 (3 oz) package instant lemon pudding mix
- ❖ ¾ cup orange juice
- ❖ ½ cup vegetable oil
- ❖ 4 eggs
- ❖ 1 teaspoon lemon extract
- ❖ 1/3 cup orange juice
- ❖ 2/3 cup white sugar
- ❖ ¼ cup butter
- ❖ ¼ cup craisins (dried cranberries)
- ❖ 2 tablespoons orange liquor

Baking Instructions:

- ❖ Combine the cake mix and lemon pudding in a large mixing bowl
- ❖ Make a well in the center and pour in ¾ cup orange juice, oil, eggs, orange liquor and lemon extract
- ❖ Beat on low speed until blended then increase speed and beat for 5 minutes
- ❖ Add the craisins and mix well
- ❖ Lightly grease a 10-inch Bundt cake pan and pour batter into cake pan
- ❖ Preheat oven to 325F and bake for 45-50 minutes
- ❖ Allow to cool in pan for 5-10 minutes, turn out onto a wire rack
- ❖ In a saucepan over medium heat, add1/3 cup of orange juice, sugar and butter for 2-3 minutes stirring.
- ❖ Drizzle sauce over cake and cut into slices
- ❖ Serve plain or with orange sorbet

Servings: 12
Per serving: 412 calories, 178 fat calories, 20g total fat, 5g saturated fat, 82mg cholesterol, 456mg sodium, 103g carbohydrate, 56g dietary fiber, 4g protein

Coconut Cake

Ingredients:

- ¾ cup shortening
- ¾ teaspoon salt
- 1½ cups white sugar
- 2 cups milk
- 3 eggs (separate yolks-beaten and whites)
- 1 teaspoon vanilla extract
- 3 cups sifted all-purpose flour
- 1 tablespoon baking soda
- 1½ teaspoons baking powder
- 1 teaspoon almond extract
- 1 cup desiccated coconut
- 1/3 cup corn syrup
- 2 tablespoons water
- ¼ teaspoon cream of tartar
- ¼ teaspoon salt
- ¾ cup white sugar
- 1 teaspoon vanilla extract

Baking Instructions:

- Add shortening, 1½ cups of sugar, egg yolks, and 1 egg white in a mixing bowl
- Beat together until well combined
- Sift flour with baking powder, salt and coconut in a large mixing bowl
- Stir flour into creamed mixture alternating with milk and the almond extract
- Lightly grease two 9 inch round layer cake pans and pour batter in them
- Preheat oven to 350F and bake for 30-40 minutes
- Allow cake to cool then remove from pans
- Add 2 egg whites, ¾ cup sugar, corn syrup, water, cream of tartar and salt in a double boiler over boiling water and beat until the mixture stands in stiff peaks

- ❖ Remove from heat, add vanilla and keep beating until it is thick enough to spread
- ❖ Spread over cooled cake and sprinkle shredded coconut on top and sides of cake
- ❖ Serve plain or with choice fruit slices

Servings: 24
Per serving: 235 calories, 77 fat calories, 9g total fat, 3g saturated fat, 28mg cholesterol, 215mg sodium, 37g carbohydrate, 1g dietary fiber, 3g protein

Guinness Chocolate and Walnut Cake

This cake can keep for a long time and it moistens as it is kept. It is best served with a spread of butter and a good strong flavored cheddar cheese.

Ingredients:

- ¼ cup butter, cut into small pieces
- 2/3 cup wholemeal flour
- ¼ cup raw or demerara sugar
- 1/3 cup walnuts, chopped
- 100 g bar of Cadbury's Bournville chocolate
- ¾ cup Guinness stout
- 1 large egg, beaten
- ½ teaspoon bicarbonate of soda
- ½ teaspoon baking powder

Baking Instructions:

- Rub the butter into the flour in a large mixing bowl, stir in the sugar and nuts
- Break up the chocolate and melt it in the Guinness in a saucepan, over a low heat
- Whisk the mixture lightly and allow mixture to cool
- Blend the mixture, egg, and rising agents into the dry ingredients
- Grease and base line with greaseproof paper a 7 inch round cake pan
- Pour mixture into baking pan and preheat oven to 350F
- Bake for 45 minutes or until a skewer inserted into the center comes out clean
- Allow cake to cool for 10-15 minutes
- Turn onto a wire rack and cut into slices
- Serve warm or cold

Servings: 6
Per serving: 307 calories, 197 fat calories, 21.9g total fat, 10.9g saturated fat, 56mg cholesterol, 119mg sodium, 22.3g carbohydrate, 3.6g dietary fiber, 5.2g protein

Lift-Me-Up Chocolate Cake

This is absolutely the best ever-chocolate cake. It will lighten up any party and bring smiles to the face of chocolate lovers; it lives up to its name.

Ingredients:

- 2 cups boiling water
- 1 cup unsweetened cocoa powder
- 2¾ cups all-purpose flour
- 2 teaspoons baking soda
- ½ teaspoon baking powder
- ½ teaspoon salt
- 1 cup butter, softened
- 2¼ cups granulated sugar
- 4 eggs
- 1½ teaspoons vanilla extract
- 1 tablespoon shaved chocolate

Baking Instructions:

- In medium bowl, add boiling water to cocoa, and whisk until smooth
- Allow mixture to cool
- Sift flour, baking soda, baking powder and salt in a bowl and set aside
- In a large mixing bowl, cream butter and sugar together until light and fluffy
- Beat in eggs one at time, and stir in vanilla extract
- Add the flour mixture, alternating with the cocoa mixture
- Grease three 9-inch round cake pans and preheat oven to 350F
- Pour mixture into baking pans
- Bake for 25-30 minutes or until a skewer inserted into the center comes out clean
- Allow cake to cool for 10-15 minutes
- Turn onto a wire rack and cut into slices
- Serve drizzled with optional chocolate syrup and sprinkle shaved chocolate on it

Servings: 12
Per serving: 428 calories, 164 fat calories, 18g total fat, 11g saturated fat, 112mg cholesterol, 508mg sodium, 64g carbohydrate, 3g dietary fiber, 7g protein

Bread and Butter Pudding

Ingredients:

- ❖ 7 slices bread
- ❖ soft butter
- ❖ 4 cups milk
- ❖ 3 eggs, slightly beaten
- ❖ ½ cup sugar
- ❖ ¼ teaspoon salt
- ❖ ½ cup raisins
- ❖ 1 teaspoon vanilla
- ❖ ½ teaspoon cinnamon

Baking Instructions:

- ❖ Preheat oven to 325°F
- ❖ Butter a 2 qt. baking dish
- ❖ Spread butter generously on one side of each slice of bread
- ❖ Line bottom and sides of baking dish with buttered bread
- ❖ Mix milk, eggs, sugar, salt, raisins, vanilla, cinnamon and pour over bread
- ❖ Place extra pieces of buttered bread on top, press down to submerge
- ❖ Let stand 10 mins, longer if bread is very dry
- ❖ Bake covered for 30 minutes, uncover and bake for additional 30 minutes
- ❖ Put under broiler, uncovered until top becomes a deep-golden crust
- ❖ Serve warm with heavy cream

Servings: 6
Per serving: 346 calories, 96 fat calories, 10.6g total fat, 5.3g saturated fat, 127mg cholesterol, 221mg sodium, 51g carbohydrate, 1.7g dietary fiber, 11.4g protein

Traditional Christmas Pudding

Ingredients:

- ❖ 1 cup self raising flour
- ❖ 4 oz fresh breadcrumbs
- ❖ 4oz ground almonds
- ❖ 1¼ lb. soft dark brown sugar
- ❖ 6 oz shredded suet
- ❖ 1 lb. currants
- ❖ 1 lb. sultanas
- ❖ 1 lb. raisins
- ❖ 2 teaspoon ground cinnamon
- ❖ 1 teaspoon ground coriander
- ❖ 1 teaspoon ground nutmeg
- ❖ 1 teaspoon ground allspice
- ❖ 1 teaspoon salt
- ❖ 6 eggs
- ❖ 1 orange
- ❖ 1 lemon
- ❖ 6 tablespoons brandy
- ❖ 1 cup brown ale

Baking Instructions:

- ❖ Add flour, breadcrumbs, ground almonds, sugar, suet, dried fruits, spices and salt in a large mixing bowl, mixing thoroughly.
- ❖ Beat the eggs in a separate bowl
- ❖ Grate the rinds and squeeze the juice from the orange and lemon
- ❖ Stir in the eggs, fruit rinds, juices, brandy and brown ale to the flour mixture
- ❖ Grease three 1½ pint pudding bowls
- ❖ Fill them with the mixture to within 1 inch of the top
- ❖ Cover each bowl with a greaseproof paper, folded and tucked to allow for expansion of the puddings.
- ❖ Cover the paper with an 18 in" square of muslin or foil
- ❖ Tie a length of string around the bowl to secure the covers

- ❖ Knot opposite ends of the muslin over the top of the bowl
- ❖ Arrange the puddings in a steamer
- ❖ Steam them for 6 hours, topping up the water if necessary
- ❖ Allow the puddings to cool
- ❖ Remove the muslin or foil covers and replace them with clean ones
- ❖ Store in a dry, cool place
- ❖ Steam for 3 hours during Christmas and then serve, garnished with a sprig of holly and brandy butter, brandy sauce or heavy whipped cream

Spiced Brandy Butter:

- ❖ 1 cup unsalted butter
- ❖ 1 cup granulated sugar
- ❖ 1 teaspoon ground Cinnamon
- ❖ 4 tablespoons brandy
- ❖ Cream the butter and sugar together in a mixing bowl until fluffy
- ❖ Add the cinnamon and brandy and blend thoroughly
- ❖ Serve with pudding

Servings: 12
Per serving: 859 calories, 198 fat calories, 21.9g total fat, 9.1g saturated fat, 115mg cholesterol, 473mg sodium, 153.7g carbohydrate, 7.6g dietary fiber, 11.5g protein

Christmas Cake

Ingredients:

- 1 cup raisins
- 1 cup sultanas
- 1 cup currants
- ½ cup mixed peel
- ½ cup glacé cherries, halved
- ¼ cup chopped blanched almonds (optional)
- ¼ cup ground almonds
- 1 cup wholemeal flour
- ¼ cup self raising flour
- pinch salt
- 1 teaspoon mixed spice
- ½ teaspoon grated nutmeg
- 8oz butter, softened
- 1 cup dark soft brown sugar
- 1 tablespoon treacle
- 4 medium eggs
- juice and rind of a lemon
- 3 oz brandy

Baking Instructions:

- Cream butter, sugar and treacle until very fluffy
- Beat in the eggs, one at a time, adding a spoonful of flour to prevent curdling
- Add the remaining flour, dried fruits and spices to mixture, mix well
- Stir in the lemon juice, rinds and brandy
- Spoon the mixture into a well-lined 9in round or 8in square tin
- Preheat oven to 300F and bake for 3-4 hours
- Cover cake with foil or brown paper halfway through cooking if cake is browning too quickly.
- Cool on a cake rack, cut into slices and serve

Servings: 12
Per serving: 442 calories, 179 fat calories, 19.9g total fat, 10.3g saturated fat, 111mg cholesterol, 192mg sodium, 59.9g carbohydrate, 3.5g dietary fiber, 5.9g protein

Apple Pie

Ingredients:

- ❖ 1 9 inch double crust pie pastry
- ❖ ½ cup unsalted butter
- ❖ 3 tablespoons all-purpose flour
- ❖ ¼ cup water
- ❖ ¼ cup white sugar
- ❖ ½ cup packed brown sugar
- ❖ 8 Granny Smith apples (peeled, cored and sliced)

Baking Instructions:

- ❖ Melt the butter in a large saucepan and stir in flour to form a paste
- ❖ Add water, white and brown sugar, and bring to a boil
- ❖ Reduce heat and let it simmer for 5-10 minutes
- ❖ Preheat oven to 425F
- ❖ Place the bottom crust in the 9 inch pie pan and fill with apples, mounded slightly
- ❖ Cover with a lattice work of crust
- ❖ Pour the butter mixture slowly over the crust to prevent a run-off
- ❖ Bake for 15 minutes, reduce the heat to 350F and bake for an additional 40-45 minutes or until the apples are soft
- ❖ Serve warm with a scoop of vanilla ice cream

Servings: 8
Per serving: 521 calories, 243 fat calories, 27g total fat, 11g saturated fat, 31mg cholesterol, 241mg sodium, 70g carbohydrate, 5g dietary fiber, 3g protein

Snacks

Sausage Rolls

Ingredients:

- ❖ 3 cups self raising flour
- ❖ ¼ lb. of butter
- ❖ 2 eggs
- ❖ ½ tablespoon salt
- ❖ ½ cup of water
- ❖ 1 egg yolk
- ❖ 3 lb. sausage meat
- ❖ ½ teaspoon season all
- ❖ ½ teaspoon nutmeg

Cooking Instructions:

- ❖ Add the flour, butter, eggs, water and salt together in a mixing bowl
- ❖ Mix and knead the dough
- ❖ Cover the dough and leave for 2 - 3 hours
- ❖ Sauté sausage meat, season all and nutmeg until cooked but not brown and drain off surplus fat
- ❖ Roll the dough on a floured pastry board about 1 inch thick
- ❖ Cut the dough into rectangular strips 2- 3 inches wide
- ❖ Scoop some of the sausage meat on one end of each dough strip
- ❖ Roll the dough strip around the meat in a tube-like fashion and trim off both ends so that the meat is slightly visible
- ❖ Arrange rolls on a baking sheet and pre-heat oven to 375 F
- ❖ Brush some egg white on the sausage rolls and bake until slightly brown
- ❖ Serve on a platter garnished with some greens

Servings: 15
Per serving: 411 calories, 217 fat calories, 24.2g total fat, 6.8g saturated fat, 70mg cholesterol, 1053mg sodium, 28.2g carbohydrate, 3.2g dietary fiber, 20.4g protein

Fish Rolls

Ingredients:

- ❖ 3 cups self raising flour
- ❖ ¼ lb. of butter
- ❖ 2 eggs
- ❖ ½ tablespoon salt
- ❖ ½ cup of water
- ❖ 1 egg yolk
- ❖ 3 lb. fish fillet, any variety
- ❖ ½ teaspoon season all
- ❖ ½ teaspoon fish sauce
- ❖ ½ cup garden peas

Cooking Instructions:

- ❖ Add the flour, butter, eggs, water and salt together in a mixing bowl
- ❖ Mix and knead the dough
- ❖ Cover the dough and leave for 2 - 3 hours
- ❖ Stir fry fish, garden peas, season all and nutmeg on medium high for 5 minutes
- ❖ Roll the dough on a floured pastry board about 1 inch thick
- ❖ Cut the dough into rectangular strips 2- 3 inches wide
- ❖ Scoop some of the fish mixture on one end of each dough strip
- ❖ Roll the dough strip around the meat in a tube-like fashion and trim off both ends so that the filling is slightly visible
- ❖ Arrange rolls on a baking sheet and pre-heat oven to 375 F
- ❖ Brush some egg white on the sausage rolls and bake until slightly brown
- ❖ Serve on a platter garnished with some greens

Servings: 15
Per serving: 258 calories, 77 fat calories, 8.5g total fat, 4.3g saturated fat, 100mg cholesterol, 1171mg sodium, 20.1g carbohydrate, 1g dietary fiber, 25.1g protein

Fish Cakes

Ingredients:

- 1 lb. 9 oz potatoes, peeled and chopped
- 1 lb. 9 oz Cod fillet
- 1 pint milk
- ½ pack parsley, finely chopped
- Salt and freshly ground black pepper to taste
- 1oz plain flour
- 2 large eggs, beaten
- 4oz breadcrumbs
- 4 cups vegetable oil for frying
- Lemon Wedges to garnish

For the green herb sauce:

- 1oz butter
- 3 tablespoon cornflour mixed with 3 tablespoon water
- 1oz capers
- 1oz gherkins
- 2 tablespoon parsley, chopped
- 2 spring onions, chopped

Cooking Instructions:

- Cook in salted water for 15-20 minutes until tender, drain and mash
- Place fish in a saucepan, add the milk and bring to a boil
- Remove saucepan from the heat, drain and reserve the milk
- Allow fish to cool a little, remove the skin and bones, flake the fish
- Combine potatoes, fish, seasonings and parsley in a large mixing bowl
- Shape into 8 cakes
- Roll each cake in flour, then dip in the beaten egg and finally the breadcrumbs
- Heat a thin layer of oil in a large, non-stick skillet over medium heat

- ❖ Fry the fish cakes for 5minutes on each side until crispy golden, set aside
- ❖ Cook the reserved milk in a saucepan with the butter and cornflour stirring until thickened
- ❖ Add the remaining sauce ingredients, season to taste and simmer for 1-2 minutes
- ❖ Serve fish cakes warm garnished with lemon wedges, vegetables and herb sauce

Servings: 6
Per serving: 389 calories, 84 fat calories, 9.2g total fat, 4.2g saturated fat, 129mg cholesterol, 505mg sodium, 45.3g carbohydrate, 3.9g dietary fiber, 30.9g protein

Aussie Meat Pie

This pie is an Australian tradition and therefore a part of her heritage. The origin seems to be lost but the first mention of the 'pie' appeared in 1850 in the Melbourne newspaper, the Argus, which reported that the councilors were unhappy with the food served in the Chambers and preferred a 'pie' from the pub opposite. Every town in Australia sells these pies, pre-packaged or freshly baked

Ingredients:

- ❖ 1 lb. ground chuck steak
- ❖ 1 beef cube
- ❖ 1 onion, thinly sliced
- ❖ 1 teaspoon Worcestershire sauce
- ❖ 1 teaspoon salt
- ❖ 1 teaspoon pepper
- ❖ 1 cup water
- ❖ ¼ teaspoon nutmeg
- ❖ 3 teaspoon flour

Pie Base

- ❖ ¼ cup water (boiling)
- ❖ 1½ cups wholemeal flour
- ❖ ½ teaspoon salt
- ❖ ½ cup melted butter
- ❖ ¼ teaspoon baking powder
- ❖ 1 egg yolk

Cooking Instructions:

- ❖ Sauté meat and onion until well browned and drain off surplus fat
- ❖ Add crumbled stock cube, salt, pepper, nutmeg, worcestershire sauce and water
- ❖ Bring to a boil and cook covered for a 20-30 minutes on medium low
- ❖ Remove pan from heat, cool slightly and add flour to thicken
- ❖ Return to heat and stir continuously until well thickened

For the pie base

- ❖ Add boiling water to butter,
- ❖ Add flour, baking powder and salt to melted butter, mix and set aside to cool
- ❖ Roll out on a floured board and cut into round shapes with a pie cutter
- ❖ Add some of the mixture to the center of the pie base
- ❖ Fold the base over and press the edges flat together
- ❖ Brush the top of the pie with egg yolk and arrange pies on a cookie sheet
- ❖ Bake in a 375 F pre-heated oven for 25 –30 minutes or until golden brown
- ❖ Serve hot or cold

Servings: 10
Per serving: 268 calories, 166 fat calories, 18.1g total fat, 9g saturated fat, 95mg cholesterol, 390mg sodium, 14g carbohydrate, 2.4g dietary fiber, 11.5g protein

Nigerian Meat Pie

Ingredients:

- 1 lb. ground meat or beef chunks
- 2 medium-sized potatoes
- ½ cup garden green peas
- 1 beef cube
- 1 teaspoon salt
- 1 teaspoon season all
- 1 teaspoon pepper
- 1 cup water
- ¼ teaspoon nutmeg
- 3 teaspoon flour

Pie Base

- 1¼ cup water (boiling)
- 6 cups flour
- 1 tablespoon salt
- ½ lb. softened butter
- ½ teaspoon baking powder
- 2 egg yolks

Cooking Instructions:

- Cut the potatoes into very small cubes
- Sauté meat until well browned and drain off surplus fat
- Add crumbled stock cube, salt, pepper, season all, nutmeg and water
- Add the potatoes and garden peas; bring to a boil and cook for a few minutes
- Remove pan from heat, cool slightly and add flour to thicken
- Return to heat and stir continuously until well thickened

For the pie base

- Add sifted flour, baking powder and salt to melted butter and mix thoroughly to form crumbs

- ❖ Add the egg yolk and water. Knead the dough and set aside for 2 – 3 hrs
- ❖ Roll out on a floured pastry board and cut into round shapes with a pie cutter
- ❖ Add some of the mixture to the center of the pie base
- ❖ Fold the base over and press the edges flat together with a fork
- ❖ Brush the top of the pie with egg yolk and arrange pies on a cookie sheet
- ❖ Bake in a 375 F pre-heated oven for 25 –30 minutes or until golden brown
- ❖ Serve hot or warm

Servings: 20
Per serving: 286 calories, 134 fat calories, 14.5g total fat, 7.6g saturated fat, 78mg cholesterol, 494mg sodium, 28.5g carbohydrate, 4.8g dietary fiber, 10g protein

Steak and Kidney Pie

Ingredients:

- ❖ 1½ lb. round steak
- ❖ 1 veal kidney
- ❖ 1 cup chopped onions
- ❖ 5 tablespoons butter, or margarine or tried-out steak fat
- ❖ 3½ cups beef bouillon
- ❖ 1 teaspoons salt
- ❖ ¼ teaspoon freshly ground pepper
- ❖ 1 teaspoon Worcestershire sauce
- ❖ 4 cups of wholemeal flour (for pastry)

Cooking Instructions:

- ❖ Trim fat from steak and melt in a skillet on medium heat
- ❖ Cut the steak into one inch cubes
- ❖ Remove fat from kidney and cut into small chunks
- ❖ Add butter or margarine to the skillet and sauté the onions lightly in the fat
- ❖ Stir in the flour and blend well
- ❖ Add the bouillon and stir until thickened
- ❖ Season with the salt, pepper, and Worcestershire sauce
- ❖ Add the meat and cool
- ❖ Follow the recipe for meat pie crust
- ❖ Line the bottom of a 2-quart casserole dish with pastry
- ❖ Add the filling and top with pastry
- ❖ Preheat oven to 450F and bake for 15-20 minutes
- ❖ Reduce the oven temperature to 325F and bake for 35-45 minutes

Servings: 12
Per serving: 285 calories, 82 fat calories, 9.2g total fat, 4.4g saturated fat, 72mg cholesterol, 1016mg sodium, 32.2 g carbohydrate, 1.4g dietary fiber, 18.7g protein

Sambusik (Lebanese Meat Patties)

A typical Lebanese meal starts with Mezze -- an elaborate spread of forty or fifty hors d'oeuvres or simply a salad and a bowl of nuts. Lamb is the most widely eaten type of meat in Lebanon

Ingredients:

- ¾ cup shortening, softened
- 2 ¼ cups sifted all-purpose flour
- ½ teaspoon salt
- ½ lb. chopped lamb
- 2 tablespoon chopped pine nuts
- 1 small onion chopped
- ¼ teaspoon pepper
- 2 sprigs fresh parsley, chopped
- 2 tablespoon water, milk or stock
- Fat for deep frying

Cooking Instructions:

- Mix the shortening, flour and salt together
- Add water to make a dough and knead
- Spread dough on a floured pastry board and roll out to 1/8th inch thickness
- Cut in rounds with a 3-inch cookie cutter
- Mix the meat, nuts, onions, seasonings, and parsley with the water, milk or stock
- Add a spoonful of the stuffing on ½ inch of each circle
- Turn the other half over and press the edges together, prick the tops with a fork
- Fry in deep hot fat until light brown 4-6 minutes
- Serve hot or cold with soup or salad

For a low calorie version, brush patties with milk and bake in a pre-heated oven at 350 F for 15 – 20 minutes

Servings: 6
Per serving: 725 calories, 537 fat calories, 59.5g total fat, 16g saturated fat, 43mg cholesterol, 223mg sodium, 33.7g carbohydrate, 5.9g dietary fiber, 13.5g protein

Jamaican Patties

Ingredients:

- 1/2 lb. lean ground beef
- 1 onion, finely chopped
- ½ teaspoon salt
- 1 teaspoon freshly ground black pepper
- ¼ cup water
- ¼ cup breadcrumbs
- ½ teaspoon curry powder
- ½ teaspoon dried thyme
- 2 tablespoons margarine
- ¼ teaspoon chopped Scotch Bonnet pepper
- ¼ cup beef or chicken stock
- 1 egg, beaten

Pie Base

- 1/3 cup cold water
- 2 cups wholemeal flour
- ¼ teaspoon salt
- ¼ teaspoon turmeric
- 1 teaspoon baking powder
- ½ teaspoon curry
- ¼ cup shortening
- ¼ cup margarine

Cooking Instructions:

- Melt the margarine in a large skillet and sauté the onion and Scotch Bonnet pepper for 5 minutes
- Add ground beef, salt, pepper, curry powder and thyme and stir
- Brown the meat for about 10 minutes, stirring occasionally
- Add the breadcrumbs and broth, mix thoroughly
- Cover the skillet and simmer for about 10 to 15 minutes, stirring occasionally until all the liquids have been absorbed
- Turn off the heat and set aside

For the pie base

- ❖ Sift the flour and salt into a large mixing bowl
- ❖ Cut in the shortening and margarine until crumbly
- ❖ Add cold water to make a stiff dough
- ❖ Lightly flour a pastry board and roll out the dough until about 1/8 inch thick
- ❖ Cut out 8 inch circles of rolled dough with a pie cutter
- ❖ Cover with wax paper or damp cloth until ready to use
- ❖ Uncover the dough and place 3 tablespoons of filling on half of each
- ❖ Moisten the edges of dough with water and fold the dough over the meat filling
- ❖ Press the edges closed with a fork and prick the top with a fork
- ❖ Lightly brush the pastry with a mixture of the egg and water
- ❖ Arrange patties on a lightly greased baking sheet
- ❖ Preheat oven to 400F
- ❖ Bake for 30 to 40 minutes or until the pastry is golden brown
- ❖ Serve hot or warm

Servings: 10
Per serving: 360 calories, 170 fat calories, 20g total fat, 7g saturated fat, 23mg cholesterol, 480mg sodium, 32g carbohydrate, 3g dietary fiber, 11g protein

Mincemeat

Mincemeat is a British delicacy and it will keep indefinitely if it is well capped or in jar. Brandy can be poured on top of it to improve its taste and keeping qualities

Ingredients:

- 1 lb. raisins, chopped
- 1 lb. currants
- 1 lb. mixed chopped candied peel
- 1 lb. apples (peeled, cored and chopped)
- grated zest of 3 lemons and 3 oranges
- ½ bottle brandy
- ½ bottle Madeira, port or sweet sherry
- 1 tablespoon mixed nutmeg, cloves and cinnamon
- 1 lb. brown sugar
- 1 lb. grated suet
- 1 lb. lean roast beef, chopped fine

Cooking Instructions:

- Mix the dry ingredients in a large mixing bowl
- Turn into an earthenware or glass pan, pressing down
- Pour the brandy and wine on top
- Cover with a tight fitting lid or foil to limit evaporation
- Keep in a cool place for 2 weeks, then stir well and it is ready for use
- Use it in preparing mincemeat pies

Servings: 12
Per serving: 809 calories, 345 fat calories, 38.3g total fat, 20.6g saturated fat, 57mg cholesterol, 51mg sodium, 101.7g carbohydrate, 5.3g dietary fiber, 14.3g protein

Pita Bread

This flat, round bread is yeast leavened and baked in a very hot oven. Its two layers are almost separated during baking, creating a hollow center, which can be split, making a pocket. It can be opened at one end and filled for a sandwich or cut in half for two smaller sandwiches

Ingredients:

- ❖ 2 ½ cups wholemeal flour
- ❖ 1 tablespoon sugar
- ❖ 2 teaspoon salt
- ❖ 1 packet dry yeast
- ❖ 2 tablespoon olive oil
- ❖ 1 cup hot water
- ❖ Eight 7-inch squares of aluminum foil

Cooking Instructions:

- ❖ Measure 1 cup flour into a mixing bowl and stir in the dry ingredients
- ❖ Add the oil and hot water and mix until blended for 30 seconds
- ❖ Beat vigorously with a wooden spoon for 3 minutes
- ❖ Stir in the rest of the flour ½ a cup at a time. The dough should be a rough, shaggy mass that will clean the sides of the bowl
- ❖ Turn the dough onto a lightly floured pastry board and knead with a rhythmic motion of push-turn-fold for about 5 minutes
- ❖ Preheat oven to 500F
- ❖ Divide the dough into eight piece and roll into balls, cover with wax paper or a towel, and leave for 20 minutes
- ❖ Flatten each ball into a disk on the palm of your hand
- ❖ Flatten further with a rolling pin into a disk of about 6 inches diameter, thickness of 3/16 inch
- ❖ Place each round on a prepared piece of foil on an oven rack to allow a softer heat to surround the dough
- ❖ Bake for about 8 minutes, or until they are puffed. For a browner crust, place pitas under broiler for 2 minutes
- ❖ Remove the breads from the oven and wrap in a large piece of foil paper
- ❖ The tops will fall and there will be a pocket in the center
- ❖ Serve warm with Shawarma , or let cool and freeze

Servings: 6
Per serving: 295 calories, 56 fat calories, 6.3g total fat, 0.7g saturated fat, 0mg cholesterol, 798mg sodium, 45.6g carbohydrate, 10.3g dietary fiber, 14.1g protein

Sharwama

This is a very tasty delicacy enjoyed by the Lebanese and it is becoming very popular in Nigeria. It can be made with beef, chicken or lamb meat.

Ingredients:

- ❖ 2 lb. of thin sliced Sirloin steak
- ❖ 1 cup of vinegar
- ❖ 1 teaspoon of cinnamon
- ❖ 1 teaspoon sweet pepper
- ❖ 1 teaspoon of nutmeg
- ❖ 1 pinch of cardamon
- ❖ 1 tablespoon of garlic salt to taste

Cooking Instructions:

- ❖ Add the spices, garlic and vinegar to the meat and marinade overnight
- ❖ Fry the meat in a little bit of oil until half cooked
- ❖ Turn into a casserole dish and cover with foil paper
- ❖ Bake in a preheated oven at 350 F for 20 minutes
- ❖ Leave in the oven for another 10 minutes
- ❖ Serve as warm pita bread filling garnished with some greens

Servings: 6
Per serving: 211 calories, 69 fat calories, 7.7g total fat, 2.6g saturated fat, 91mg cholesterol, 677mg sodium, 3.4g carbohydrate, 0.6g dietary fiber, 32.2g protein

Breadfruit Fries

Breadfruit is a round green-to-brownish-green fruit with a white starchy pulp and can be served like a potato or winter squash; it can be baked, boiled, fried, or roasted with or without the peel. The breadfruit tree can grow as tall as 60 feet high and it is best cooked as it begins to ripen. It can be soaked in water overnight before peeling it. Baked or roasted breadfruit can be eaten with butter, salt and pepper

Ingredients:

- ❖ 1 medium breadfruit, firm
- ❖ 1 teaspoon salt
- ❖ Canola oil for deep frying

Cooking Instructions:

- ❖ Cut the breadfruit into 2 halves and peel
- ❖ Cut into wedges and add salt to taste
- ❖ Add oil in deep fat fryer ad preheat to 350F
- ❖ Fry wedges in oil until light brown 4-6 minutes
- ❖ Allow oil to drain and turn into a platter
- ❖ Serve hot or cold with some spinach dip

Servings: 6
Per serving: 255 calories, 85 fat calories, 9.4g total fat, 0.5g saturated fat, 0mg cholesterol, 396mg sodium, 41g carbohydrate, 7.6g dietary fiber, 1.6g protein

Non – Alcoholic Beverages

Summer PineLime Kisser

Ingredients:

- ❖ 1 16oz can unsweetened pineapple juice
- ❖ 1 liter 7UP
- ❖ 4 cups ocean spray cranberry juice
- ❖ 5 limes (4 juiced, 1 sliced into thin rings: wrap each string around the finger and drop into ice cold water for garnishing)
- ❖ ½ a bag of ice cubes

Mixing Instructions:

- ❖ Chill the juices overnight in the refrigerator
- ❖ Mix the pineapple juice, 7UP and cranberry juice in a punch bowl
- ❖ Add the lime juice and mix thoroughly
- ❖ Add the ice cubes and mix well
- ❖ Serve in frosted glasses and garnish with lime strings

Coffee Punch Lift–Me-Up

Ingredients:

- ❖ 3 cups strong ice coffee
- ❖ 2 cups light whipping cream (whip 1 cup)
- ❖ 1 qt Starbucks Light ice cream (softened)
- ❖ ½ cup very fine sugar
- ❖ 2 teaspoon Bourbon vanilla extract
- ❖ ½ cup crushed pecan nuts

Mixing Instructions:

- ❖ Add the coffee, sugar, vanilla and a cup of cream in a blender and blend at a high speed
- ❖ Place softened ice cream in a punch bowl and add coffee mixture
- ❖ Whisk the mixture
- ❖ Serve in tall glasses with a dollop of whipped cream, sprinkle nuts on top

Home-made Frappuccino

Ingredients:

- ❖ ½ cup freshly brewed Starbucks espresso
- ❖ 2½ cups whole milk
- ❖ ¼ cup very fine granulated sugar
- ❖ 1 tablespoon dry pectin (optional)

Mixing Instructions:

- ❖ Add the espresso, sugar, and milk in a blender and blend at a high speed
- ❖ Whisk the mixture at a high speed
- ❖ Chill for 1 hour or more
- ❖ Serve in tall frozen glasses with a dollop of whipped cream

Cranberry Juice

Ingredients:

- ❖ 2 lb. fresh cranberries
- ❖ 3 cups of sugar
- ❖ 12 cups of water

Mixing Instructions:

- ❖ Combine cranberries, sugar and water in a 4 qt saucepan
- ❖ Bring to a boil and reduce heat to continue simmering
- ❖ Simmer until cranberries are soft
- ❖ Use a cheesecloth to strain the juice
- ❖ Refrigerate for 4 hours and serve over ice in tall glasses

Traditional Banana Milk Shake

Ingredients:

- ❖ 2 cups milk (Use skim milk for calorie watchers)
- ❖ 2 ripe bananas, diced
- ❖ 1 pint ice cream
- ❖ 1 teaspoon Vanilla extract
- ❖ Maraschino cherries

Mixing Instructions:

- ❖ Add the milk, vanilla extract, bananas and ice cream into a blender
- ❖ Blend at high speed until smooth
- ❖ Serve in tall glasses with a cherry on top

Sweet Sensations

Ingredients:

- ❖ 10 peach teabags
- ❖ 1 16oz can of unsweetened pineapple juice
- ❖ 1 cup of freshly squeezed pulp free lemon juice
- ❖ 1 liter of ginger ale
- ❖ 3 cups of freshly squeezed orange juice
- ❖ 2 cups of sugar
- ❖ 6 cups of water

Mixing Instructions:

- ❖ Boil the water and steep the teabags in it for 5 – 10 minutes and remove
- ❖ Add the sugar and mix well, then chill for about 5 hours
- ❖ In a punch bowl, add the chilled tea and the juices and stir
- ❖ Add the ginger ale and some ice cubes and stir
- ❖ Serve immediately in tall frosted glasses

Hawaiian Exotic Fruit Punch

Ingredients:

- 4 cups orange juice
- 4 cups guava juice
- 4 cups pineapple juice
- 1 cup ginger ale
- ½ cup grenadine, red

Mixing Instructions:

- Mix frozen juice concentrates following directions on cans
- Add all juices together in a punch bowl, chill for about 5 hours
- Add the ginger ale, grenadine and some ice cubes and stir
- Serve immediately in tall frosted glasses

Warm Exotic and Spicy Autumn Punch

Ingredients:

- ❖ 2 navel oranges
- ❖ 6 cups apple juice
- ❖ 3 tablespoons lemon juice
- ❖ 2¼ cups pineapple juice
- ❖ 8 whole cloves
- ❖ 1 cinnamon stick
- ❖ ¼ teaspoon ground nutmeg
- ❖ ¼ cup honey

Mixing Instructions:

- ❖ Stud the 2 navel oranges with cloves
- ❖ Preheat oven to 350F and bake for 30 minutes
- ❖ Add the apple juice and cinnamon stick in a large saucepan and bring to a boil
- ❖ Reduce heat and simmer for 5 minutes
- ❖ Remove from heat, stir in the nutmeg, honey, lemon juice and pineapple juice
- ❖ Serve hot in a punch bowl with the 2 clove-studded baked navel oranges afloat

Creamy Orange

Ingredients:

- ❖ 1 cup milk
- ❖ 1 cup ice water
- ❖ 1 (6 oz) can frozen orange juice concentrate
- ❖ 12 cubes ice cubes
- ❖ ¼ teaspoon vanilla extract
- ❖ 1/8 cup white sugar

Mixing Instructions:

- ❖ Combine milk, water, orange juice concentrate, ice cubes, vanilla and sugar in a blender
- ❖ Blend at a high speed until smooth
- ❖ Serve immediately in tall frosted glasses and enjoy with a straw

Absolute Lemonade

Ingredients:

- ❖ 1¾ cups white sugar
- ❖ 8 cups water
- ❖ 1½ cups lemon juice

Mixing Instructions:

- ❖ Combine sugar and 1 cup water in a small saucepan
- ❖ Bring to boil and stir to dissolve sugar
- ❖ Allow to cool to room temperature, cover and refrigerate until chilled
- ❖ Remove seeds from lemon juice, but leave pulp
- ❖ In pitcher, stir together chilled syrup, lemon juice and remaining 7 cups water
- ❖ Add some ice cubes or chill for 2 hours
- ❖ Serve in tall frosted glasses and enjoy with a straw

Berry Colada

Ingredients:

- ❖ 2 (46 oz) bottles cranberry-raspberry juice
- ❖ 1 (32 oz) bottle pina colada mix
- ❖ 2 liters raspberry ginger ale soda

Mixing Instructions:

- ❖ Combine cranberry-raspberry juice with the pina colada mix in a large plastic container
- ❖ Freeze juice overnight
- ❖ Remove from freezer 30 minutes prior to serving
- ❖ Place frozen slush in a punch bowl and slowly add raspberry ginger ale
- ❖ Serve in tall frosted glasses and enjoy with a straw

Cappuccino Cooler

Ingredients:

- ❖ 1½ cups cold coffee
- ❖ 1½ cups chocolate ice cream
- ❖ ¼ cup chocolate syrup
- ❖ crushed ice
- ❖ 1 cup whipped cream

Mixing Instructions:

- ❖ Combine coffee, ice cream and chocolate syrup in a blender
- ❖ Blend mixture until smooth
- ❖ Pour over crushed ice
- ❖ Serve in tall glasses and garnish with a dollop of whipped cream

Honey and Fruit Smoothie

Ingredients:

- ❖ 1 (10 oz) package frozen mixed berries
- ❖ 1 (15 oz) can sliced peaches, drained (or pears)
- ❖ 2 tablespoons honey

Mixing Instructions:

- ❖ Combine frozen fruit, canned fruit and honey in a blender
- ❖ Blend mixture until smooth
- ❖ Serve in tall frosted glasses

Seasonings and Spices

Traditional Pepper Soup Seasoning

Grind in a coffee grinder

- ❖ 1oz atariko
- ❖ 1oz uda
- ❖ 1oz gbafilo
- ❖ 1oz ginger (dried)
- ❖ 1oz rigije
- ❖ 1oz uyayak

Pepper Soup Substitute Seasoning

The traditional spice may not be easily available in some countries but this can be grinded and used as pepper soup spice. It gives an almost similar taste to the authentic one.

- ❖ 1oz aniseed
- ❖ 1oz aniseed pepper
- ❖ ½ oz cloves
- ❖ 1oz coriander seeds
- ❖ 1oz cumin seeds
- ❖ 1oz allspice
- ❖ 1oz dried ginger
- ❖ 1oz tamarind pods
- ❖ 1oz fennel seeds

Curry Powder

Spice seeds can be bought in bulk at most health food stores. This curry powder may be stored in a cool dark place for up to several months.

- ❖ 4 teaspoon coriander seeds
- ❖ 4 teaspoon cumin seeds
- ❖ 2 teaspoon fenugreek seeds
- ❖ 2 bay leaves
- ❖ 1 teaspoon black peppercorns
- ❖ 1 teaspoon ground turmeric
- ❖ 1 teaspoon pure chili powder

- ❖ Dry roast the coriander, cumin and fenugreek in a skillet for about 2 minutes until lightly browned.
- ❖ Grind in a spice grinder or coffee grinder with the bay leaves and peppercorns.
- ❖ Shake with the turmeric and chili powder in a small, airtight container. This will give about 4 tablespoons of curry.

Index

A

America
  Apple Pie, 106
  Broccoli Salad, 44
  Coconut Cake, 98
  Coffee Punch Lift-Me-Up, 128
  Cranberry Juice, 130
  Creamy Garlic Mashed Potato, 78
  Grilled Salmon Steak, 72
  Lemony Pound Cake, 96
  Lift-Me-Up Chocolate Cake, 101
  Slow Cooking Barbecue Steak, 74
  Slow Cooking Meat Loaf, 73
  Slow Cooking Tasty Leg-of-Lamb,
    75
  Sweet Honey Bun Cake, 94
  Tender and Spicy Baby Back Ribs,
    76
Antipasto
  Mozzarella, Tomato and Basil
    Bruschetta, 21
Australia
  Aussie Meat Pie, 113
  Sausage Rolls, 109

B

Banana
  Moist Signature Banana Pound Cake,
    93
  Traditional Banana Milk Shake, 131
Barbecue
  Honey and Garlic Ribs, 77
  Slow Cooking Barbecue Steak, 74
  Tender and Spicy Baby Back Ribs,
    76
Beans
  Cowpea Fritters (Akara), 67
  Steamed Bean Cakes (Moin-Moin),
    65
  Traditional Nigerian Bean Casserole
    (Ewa Riro), 69
Beef
  Aussie Meat Pie, 113
  Hot & Spicy Beef Satay (Suya), 24
  Jamaican Patties, 119
  Mincemeat, 121
  Nigerian Meat Pie, 115
  Ogbono, 85
  Shepherd's Pie, 79

  Slow Cooking Barbecue Steak, 74
  Slow Cooking Meat Loaf, 73
Brandy
  Mincemeat, 121
Bread
  Bread and Butter Pudding, 102
  Currant Loaves, 20
  Mozarrella, Tomato & Basil
    Bruschetta, 21
  Pita Bread, 122
  Slow Cooking Meat Loaf, 73
Britain
  Bread and Butter Pudding, 102
  Christmas Cake, 105
  Currant Loaves, 20
  Fish Cakes, 111
  Fisherman's Pie, 80
  Guinness Chocolate and Walnut
    Cake, 100
  Mincemeat, 121
  Shepherd's Pie, 79
  Steak and Kidney Pie, 117
  Traditional Christmas Pudding, 103
Broth
  French Onion Soup, 36
  Fried Rice, 53
  Minestrone Soup, 28
  Tomato Soup, 37
  Traditional Chicken & Vegetable
    Soup, 27
Brûlée
  Coffee - Brandy Creme Brûlée, 90
  Creme Brulee Classic, 89

C

Cake
  Christmas Cake, 105
  Coconut Cake, 98
  Guinness Chocolate and Walnut
    Cake, 100
  Heavenly Pound Cake, 95
  Lemony Pound Cake, 96
  Lift-Me-Up Chocolate Cake, 101
  Moist Signature Banana Pound Cake,
    93
  Signature Rum Carrot Cake, 92
  Sweet Honey Bun Cake, 94
  Tiramisu', 91
  Traditional Christmas Pudding, 103
Carribean Islands
  Curry Goat, 81

Curry Pork, 82
Curry Prawn, 83
Mozarrella, Tomato & Basil
    Bruschetta, 21
Pita Bread, 122
Slow Cooking Meat Loaf, 73
Britain
Bread and Butter Pudding, 102
Steak and Kidney Pie, 117
Traditional Christmas Pudding, 103
Broth
French Onion Soup, 36
Fried Rice, 53
Minestrone Soup, 28
Tomato Soup, 37
Traditional Chicken & Vegetable
    Soup, 27
Brûlée
Coffee - Brandy Creme Brûlée, 90
Creme Brulee Classic, 89

C

Cake
Christmas Cake, 105
Coconut Cake, 98
Guinness Chocolate and Walnut
    Cake, 100
Heavenly Pound Cake, 95
Lemony Pound Cake, 96
Lift-Me-Up Chocolate Cake, 101
Moist Signature Banana Pound Cake,
    93
Signature Rum Carrot Cake, 92
Sweet Honey Bun Cake, 94
Tiramisu', 91
Traditional Christmas Pudding, 103
Carribean Islands
Curry Goat, 81
Curry Pork, 82
Curry Prawn, 83
Fried Plantain Pizza, 18
Jamaican Patties, 119
Jerk Chicken, 70
Carrot
Signature Rum Carrot Cake, 92
Casserole
Traditional Nigerian Bean Casserole
    (Ewa Riro), 69
Cheese
Everything Lasagna, 60
French Onion Soup, 36
Fried Plantain Pizza, 18
Italian Hand Tossed Salad, 42

Christmas Cake, 105
Currant Loaves, 20
Fish Cakes, 111
Fisherman's Pie, 80
Guinness Chocolate and Walnut
    Cake, 100
Mincemeat, 121
Shepherd's Pie, 79
Mozzarella, Tomato and Basil
    Bruschetta, 21
Chicken
Chicken Caesar-Cranberry Pasta
    Salad, 47
Jerk Chicken, 70
Sharwama, 123
Snow Peas and Chicken Vinaigrette
    Pasta Salad, 48
Tangy Chicken, 71
Chocolate
Guinness Chocolate and Walnut
    Cake, 100
Lift-Me-Up Chocolate Cake, 101
Christmas
Christmas Cake, 105
Traditional Christmas Pudding, 103
Coffee
Cappuccino Cooler, 138
Coffee - Brandy Creme Brûlée, 90
Coffee Punch Lift-Me-Up, 128
Home-made Frappuccino, 129
Tiramisu', 91
Coleslaw
Tangy Coleslaw, 46
Cranberries
Berry Colada, 137
Chicken Caesar-Cranberry Pasta
    Salad, 47
Cranberry Juice, 130
Italian Hand Tossed Salad, 42
Summer PineLime Kisser, 127
Tangy Coleslaw, 46
Very Fruity Salad, 41
Currant
Currant Loaves, 20
Curry
Curry Goat, 81
Curry Pork, 82
Curry Prawn, 83

E

Eggs
Boiled Yam & Scrambled Eggs, 57
Coffee - Brandy Creme Brûlée, 90

Creme Brulee Classic, 89
Scotch Egg, 19
Tiramisu', 91

F

Fish
    Fish Cakes, 111
    Fish Pepper Soup, 31
    Fish Rolls, 110
    Fisherman's Pie, 80
    Grilled Salmon Steak, 72
Flour
    Chin-Chin, 22
    Puff-Puff (Nigerian Dough Nut), 23
France
    Coffee - Brandy Creme Brulee, 78
    Creme Brulee, 77
    French Onion Soup, 36
Fries
    Breadfruit Fries, 124
Fruit
    Hawaiian Exotic Fruit Punch, 133
Fruits
    Very Fruity Salad, 41

G

Gambia
    Jollof Rice, 55
    Tangy Chicken, 71
Garlic
    Creamy Garlic Mashed Potato, 78
Ghana
    Jollof Rice, 55
Goat
    Curry Goat, 81
    Goat Pepper Soup, 29

K

Kidney
    Everything Pepper Soup, 33
    Steak and Kidney Pie, 117

L

Lamb
    Sambusik (Lebanese Meat Patties),
        118
    Sharwama, 123
    Shepherd's Pie, 79

Guava
    Hawaiian Exotic Fruit Punch, 133
Guinness
    Guinness Chocolate and Walnut
        Cake, 100

H

Hawaii
    Hawaiian Exotic Fruit Punch, 133
Hen
    Guinea Hen Pepper Soup, 30

I

Ice Cream
    Cappuccino Cooler, 138
    Coffee Punch Lift-Me-Up, 128
    Traditional Banana Milk Shake, 131
Italy
    Italian Hand Tossed Salad, 42
    Low Calories Clam Chowder, 34
    Minestrone Soup, 28
    Mixed Greens Salad, 43
    Mozzarella, Tomato and Basil
        Bruschetta, 21
    Pesto Spaghetti with Meatballs, 63
    Prawns and Artichoke Pasta Salad,
        49
    Seafood Bisque, 35
    Snow Peas & Chicken Vinaigrette
        Pasta Salad, 48
    Spaghetti with Minced Meat, 64
    Spinach & Sun-Dried Tomato Pasta
        Salad, 45
    Tiramisu, 79
    Vegetable Lasagna, 59

    Slow Cooking Tasty Leg-of-Lamb,
        75
Lasagna
    Everything Lasagna, 60
    Vegetable Lasagna, 59
Lebanon
    Pita Bread, 122
    Sharwarma, 109
Lebanon
    Sambusik (Lebanese Meat Patties),
        118
Lemon
    Absolute Lemonade, 136
Lime
    Summer PineLime Kisser, 127

M

Mascarpone
   Tiramisu', 91
Melon
   Melon Stew (Egunsi), 62
Milk Shake
   Traditional Banana Milk Shake, 131

N

Nigeria
   Boiled Yam & Scrambled Eggs, 57
   Breadfruit Fries, 124
   Broiled Plantain (Boli), 17
   Chin-Chin, 22
   Corned Beef Sauce, 58
   Cowpea Fritters (Akara), 67
   Edikan-ikong, 84
   Everything Pepper Soup, 33
   Fish Pepper Soup, 31
   Fish Rolls, 110
   Fried Plantain Pizza, 18
   Fried Rice, 53
   Fried Yam & Pepper Dip (Dun-Dun
      & Ata), 54
   Goat Pepper Soup, 29
   Guinea Hen Pepper Soup, 30
   Hot & Spicy Beef Satay (Suya), 24
   Jollof Rice, 55
   Melon Stew (Egunsi), 62
   Nigerian Meat Pie, 115
   Ogbono, 85
   Oxtail Pepper Soup, 32
   Puff-Puff (Nigerian Dough Nut), 23
   Sausage Rolls, 109
   Steamed Bean Cakes (Moin-Moin),
      65
   Tangy Chicken, 71
   Traditional Nigerian Bean Caserole
      (Ewa Riro), 69
   Yam Fritters (Ojojo), 68
   Yam Pottage (Asaro), 61
   Hot & Spicy Beef Satay (Suya), 24
   Oxtail Pepper Soup, 32
Pie
   Apple Pie, 106
Pies
   Aussie Meat Pie, 113
   Fisherman's Pie, 80
   Jamaican Patties, 119
   Nigerian Meat Pie, 115
   Sambusik (Lebanese Meat Patties),
      118

Yam Stew (Ikokore), 86

O

Onion
   French Onion Soup, 36
Orange
   Creamy Orange, 135
   Hawaiian Exotic Fruit Punch, 133
   Warm Exotic and Spicy Autumn, 134
Oxtail
   Oxtail Pepper Soup, 32

P

Pacific Rim
   Honey and Garlic Ribs, 77
Pasta
   Chicken Caesar Cranberry Pasta
      Salad, 47
   Everything Lasagna, 60
   Pesto Sphaghetti with Meatballs, 63
   Prawns & Artichoke Pasta Salad, 49
   Snow Peas and Chicken Vinaigrette
      Pasta Salad, 48
   Spaghetti with Minced Meat, 64
   Spinach & Sun Dried Tomato Pasta
      Salad, 32
   Vegetable Lasagna, 59
Patties
   Jamaican Patties, 119
   Sambusik (Lebanese Meat Patties),
      118
Peaches
   Honey and Fruit Smoothie, 139
Pepper
   Everything Pepper Soup, 33
   Fish Pepper Soup, 31
   Fried Yam & Pepper Dip (Dun-Dun
      & Ata), 54
   Goat Pepper Soup, 29
   Guinea Hen Pepper Soup, 30

   Shepherd's Pie, 79
   Steak and Kidney Pie, 117
Pina Colada
   Berry Colada, 137
Pineapple
   Hawaiian Exotic Fruit Punch, 133
   Summer PineLime Kisser, 127
   Sweet Sensations, 132
   Warm Exotic and Spicy Autumn, 134
Plantain

Broiled Plantain - Boli, 17
Fried Plantain Pizza, 18
Pork
    Curry Pork, 82
    Honey and Garlic Ribs, 77
    Tender and Spicy Baby Back Ribs,
      76
Potato
    Creamy Garlic Mashed Potato, 78
Prawns
    Curry Prawn, 83
Pudding
    Bread and Butter Pudding, 102
    Traditional Christmas Pudding, 103
Pumpkin
    Edikan-ikong, 84
Punch
    Hawaiian Exotic Fruit Punch, 133
    Warm Exotic and Spicy Autumn, 134

R

Raspberries
    Berry Colada, 137
Ribs
    Honey and Garlic Ribs, 77
    Tender and Spicy Baby Back Ribs,
      76
Rice
    Fried Rice, 53
    Jollof Rice, 55
Rum
    Moist Signature Banana Pound Cake,
      93
    Signature Rum Carrot Cake, 92
    Tiramisu', 91

S

Salad
    Broccoli Salad, 44
    Chicken Caesar Cranberry Pasta
      Salad, 47
    Italian Hand Tossed Salad, 42
    Mixed Greens Salad, 43
    Prawns & Artichoke Pasta Salad, 49
    Snow Peas & Chicken Vinaigrette
      Pasta Salad, 48
    Spinach & Sun-Dried Tomato Pasta
      Salad, 45
    Seafood Bisque, 35
    Tomato Soup, 37

Tangy Coleslaw, 46
Very Fruity Salad, 41
Sausage
    Sausage Rolls, 109
    Scotch Egg, 19
Scotland
    Scotch Egg, 19
Seafood
    Curry Prawn, 83
    Low Calories Clam Chowder, 34
    Ogbono, 85
    Prawns and Artichoke Pasta Salad,
      49
    Seafood Bisque, 35
Signature
    Absolute Lemonade, 136
    Berry Colada, 137
    Cappuccino Cooler, 138
    Chicken Caesar-Cranberry Pasta
      Salad, 47
    Creamy Orange, 135
    Everything Lasagna, 60
    Heavenly Pound Cake, 95
    Home-made Frappuccino, 129
    Honey and Fruit Smoothie, 139
    Moist Signature Banana Pound Cake,
      93
    Signature Rum Carrot Cake, 92
    Summer PineLime Kisser, 127
    Sweet Sensations, 132
    Tangy Coleslaw, 46
    Tomato Soup, 37
    Traditional Banana Milk Shake, 131
    Traditional Chicken & Vegetable
      Soup, 27
    Very Fruity Salad, 41
    Warm Exotic and Spicy Autumn
      Punch, 120
Smoothie
    Honey and Fruit Smoothie, 139
Soup
    Everything Pepper Soup, 33
    Fish Pepper Soup, 31
    French Onion Soup, 36
    Goat Pepper Soup, 29
    Guinea Hen Pepper Soup, 30
    Low Calories Clam Chowder, 34
    Minestrone Soup, 28
    Oxtail Pepper Soup, 32

    Traditional Chicken & Vegetable
      Soup, 27
Spinach

Italian Hand Tossed Salad, 42
Steak
    Sharwama, 123
    Steak and Kidney Pie, 117
Stew
    Corned Beef Sauce, 58
    Edikan-ikong, 84
    Melon Stew (Egunsi), 62
    Ogbono, 85
    Yam Stew (Ikokore), 86
Suet
    Mincemeat, 121

T

Tea
    Sweet Sensations, 132
Tomato
    Spinach and Sun-Dried Tomato Pasta
        Salad, 45
    Tomato Soup, 37

V

Vegetables

Breadfruit Fries, 124
Broccoli Salad, 44
Tomato Soup, 37
Traditional Chicken & Vegetable
    Soup, 27
Vegetable Lasagna, 59

W

Walnut
    Guinness Chocolate and Walnut
        Cake, 100
Waterleaf
    Edikan-ikong, 84

Y

Yam
    Boiled Yam & Scrambled Eggs, 57
    Fried Yam & Pepper Dip, 54
    Yam Fritters (Ojojo), 68
    Yam Pottage (Asaro), 61
    Yam Stew (Ikokore), 86

Conversion Chart

TEMPERATURES

°C	°F	Gas Mark	USA
70	150	¼	Cool
80	175	¼	Cool
100	200	½	Cool
110	225	½	Cool
130	250	1	V Slow
140	275	1	V Slow
150	300	2	Slow
170	325	3	Moderate
180	350	4	Moderate
190	375	5	Moderately Hot
200	400	6	Fairly Hot
220	425	7	Hot
230	450	8	Very Hot
240	475	8	Very Hot
250	500	9	Extremely Hot
270	525	9	Extremely Hot
290	550	9	Extremely Hot

COMMON INGREDIENTS CONVERSION

Ingredients	USA	Metric	Imperial
Flour	1 Cup	140g	5oz
Castor & Granulated Sugar	1 Cup	225g	8oz
Castor & Granulated Sugar	2 Level Tablespoons	30g	1oz
Brown Sugar	1 Cup	170g	6oz
Butter/ Margarine/ Lard	1 Cup	225g	8oz
Sultanas/ raisins	1 Cup	200g	7oz
Currants	1 Cup	140g	5oz
Ground Almonds	1 Cup	110g	4oz
Golden Syrup	1 Cup	340g	12oz
Uncooked Rice	1 Cup	200g	7oz
Grated Cheese	1 Cup	110g	4oz
Butter	1 Stick	110g	4oz

DRY WEIGHT MEASUREMENTS

Metric	Imperial
15g	½ oz
30g	1 oz
90g	2 oz
125g	3 oz
115g	4 oz (¼ lb.)
185g	5 oz
220g	6 oz
250g	7 oz
280g	8 oz (½ lb.)
315g	9 oz
345g	10 oz
375g	11 oz
410g	12 oz (¾ lb.)

VOLUME MEASUREMENTS

Metric	Imperial
30ml	1 fluid oz
60ml	2 fluid oz
100ml	3 fluid oz
125ml	4 fluid oz
150ml	5 fluid oz (¼ pint or 1 gill)
190ml	6 fluid oz
250ml	8 fluid oz
300ml	10 fluid oz
500ml	16 fluid oz
600ml	20 fluid oz (1 pint)

CUP AND SPOON CONVERSION

Australian	UK/US
Australian	*UK/US*
1 Tablespoon	3 teaspoons
2 Tablespoons	¼ cup
1/4 cup	1/3 cup
1/3 cup	½ cup
1/2 cup	2/3 cup
2/3 cup	¾ cup
3/4 cup	1 cup
1 cup	1¼ cups

PAN SIZES

U.S.	Metric
8" cake pan	20 x 4 cm sandwich or cake tin
9" cake pan	23 x 3.5 cm sandwich or cake tin
11" x 7" baking pan	28 x 18 cm baking tin
13" x 9" baking pan	32.5 x 23 cm baking tin
15" x 10" baking pan	38 x 25.5 cm baking tin (Swiss roll tin)
2 qt rectangular baking dish	30 x 19 cm baking dish
1½ qt baking dish	1.5 liter baking dish
2 qt baking dish	2 liter baking dish
9" pie plate	22 x 4 or 23 x 4 cm pie plate
7" or 8" springform pan	18 or 20 cm springform
9" x 5" loaf pan	23 x 13 cm or 2 lb. narrow loaf or pate tin